The boy from the sewing room would never be the man he is today had it not been for you.

Thank you

# THE RIGHTING MOMENT

This book is of fantasy and is a fiction.
No character depicted relates to any living, or dead, with the
exception of God who is exempt from both.

A novel by:

ANDREW S FINCHAM

ISBN: 1500601578
ISBN 13: 9781500601577

We don't see things as they are,
we see them as we are.

Anais Nin

# PREFACE

You only find your one true "love of a lifetime" once in a lifetime... redundant and true. And while love is genuinely everything, just like everything, love is a choice. You may choose to be that silver-haired couple seated next to one another on the train, still laughing after all of those years. Or, you can choose to know that it was real because the hollow ache of its absence is carried with you for the remainder of your days; always there...always eager to remind you.

I do not remember falling in love with her. When I reflect on this, the only conclusion I can come to is that I just always have. Of course, I've heard myself say, "I love you" to other people. But it was different with the two of us right from the beginning. It wasn't like we met and fell in love; we met again and already were. We just had to remember.

She would say the same too, even now, if you were to ask her. What we found together was transcendent in some way. Our bond has affected us both on a level that is truly spiritual.

How then could it have ended so poorly, and why has its loss lingered on? It is simple really; it comes back to those choices.

From the journal of:
Nicholas Morrison
February Fourth

# Chapter 1

I am shocked awake; it is as if a safe has fallen from a window high above and landed just behind my head. Somewhere off in the distance is a bellow as loud as thunder, only too short in duration and carrying no resonant weight. I reach back clumsily and open the mosquito net, searching inside of the rainfly for my pack. Following the bag's familiar lines, I find an outside pocket and inside is my handheld GPS.

I'd charged the GPS earlier with a portable solar pad that rolls away neatly into it's own pouch on the pack's shoulder strap. The display glares at me brightly, and I squint painfully through my eyelashes to focus on the screen. It is three o'clock in the morning exactly...the witches' hour.

Outside the air is still. I can hear birds flying through the treetops above me. In a small hollow below, a herd of deer moves quickly as brittle leaves sound dryly beneath their hooves. I trace the zipper by my side down to my knees and push out from the chrysalis of my sleeping bag.

It is colder than it has been at any point along the trail so far. The sky is clear and bright; the pregnant moon is in full season. I look up through a collage made by a sweet gum. Its star shaped leaves and hanging witches burrs form a mosaic of great wonder. The cosmos beyond backlights this image with clouds of far off worlds, eagerly wanting to be seen.

The serenity is overwhelming. The lights from above play reflections through the crystals of the first hard frost and seem almost to sing to me in some way. It's like the toy that had unwound its song once and soothed me as I lay in my crib.

As happens when the trail is truly beautiful, I find myself thinking of Ava. I wish I could share this morning with her, hear her laugh, smell her skin. Closing my eyes I can see her as if she is laying next to me, propped up on her elbows, our smiles so close they almost touch. The sun coming through the window at our feet illuminates tiny whispers of blonde hair at the base of her spine. I trace the lines of her back with the lightest touch of my fingers across her naked skin.

She shivers and smiles at me all the more. I can still feel her hand holding my thigh, almost touching me. Together we had learned to feel truly alive right through life's little deaths. It is in the memories of such dizzying heights that I remain forever lost.

We'd known each other since we were children, and she could be a real handful. She could also laugh in the most contagious way, and she robbed me of both my inhibitions, and of my ability to breathe. A quality she'd always possessed in my eyes. She, quite plainly, took my breath away.

She and I first explored love as teenagers. In an art class together I'd made her feel awkward, as I was unable to take my eyes off of her. In times when the class had lengthy stretches of freedom for the students to develop their talents, I would sit by her and softly touch the skin of her neck and shoulders.

She said she felt an energy pass between us that thrilled her unlike anything she'd known before. I'd trace the tips of my fingers across her and found such simple joy in the contact we shared. Twenty-two years later, when we met again, she told me then that the charge was still there, and unlike anything she had known since.

I doubt if ever two people had found love together and been able to explore higher levels of connectivity between their very souls. I doubt, as well, if two people had ever created a landscape between themselves so filled with petty fears, and the angst it generated as a result. We had always said we had never known real love before the one we had found together. These months later the empty place she had once filled felt like the death of a loved one—permanent and heavy.

Now I reach inside of my tent and, from the small hammock stitched into its peak, I grab one of two tangerines. It is over ripened and pulls cleanly from its peel. I break it into individual sections between my fingers as I sit on the edge of the lean-to. Off to the northeast I see the sodium glow of a town's streetlights silhouetting the spine of the mountains.

I have been keeping fairly constant fixes upon my position as I proceed along the trail. I was an open ocean navigator, a deck watch officer certified on large seafaring ships. Keeping running tabs of position is easy by comparison with landmarks as obvious as mountains. According to the fixes I have worked out in my mind, I can't place a town where I see one.

I make a mental note to consult the GPS in the morning and correct my dead reckoning. It is certainly a quirk of the way the trail has gone through a long, lazy series of curves between mountains larger than what I'm accustomed to. Finishing my last section of fruit, I crawl back into my nylon cocoon and sleep seems to be waiting there for me already.

A yellow dwarf named The Sun lives no more.

Its shell, cooling in a vast empty abyss, hardens into paper fine layers of ash. Its last energy spent it expands slowly like a child's Pharaoh's Snake burning on the sidewalk on the Fourth of July.

In an ochre vacuum it hangs. There is a sound of consumption, like a long, slow-peeling wave breaking across an isolated shoreline.

A black mass lets loose its last breath illuminated tightly by a bright yellow sky, which surrounds it.

ᴧ

This is my first thought when I open my eyes and see the last of my tangerines hanging in the hammock over my face. The sun shines brightly outside, and the glow through the tent is indeed like a yellow sky. But as I peel the dead star and pop a piece in my mouth, I have to marvel at what a refreshing way it is to start a day. To be thinking freely and clearly, my imagination is unleashed after so long being high centered on a wet, rotten log.

I sit on the edge of the lean-to and lace my boots onto my feet after retrieving my socks from the nearby bush. As I bend over tightening the laces, a ruffed grouse begins drumming not fifty yards away. At first it surprises me. Then, as the staccato of his wing beats increases, I simply laugh knowing that he, too, is feeling the need of a companion. His rhythm accelerates, like a kid with a card in the spokes of his bicycle building up speed down a steep driveway.

The drumming ends as suddenly as it begins, and I see the eager suitor as he disappears under the rhododendrons covering the glade I'm camping in.

I head off east by northeast, following the timeworn trail onward, always toward Pamola who is certainly waiting with a gale from his own wings to greet me. My pace is quick, and my steps feel fresh. I am moving across the terrain with an easy grace I have not felt before. It's as if I want to run. No… I want to skip.

Yet again the feelings come as memories, and I find myself reflecting upon the weight that sits constantly on my chest. Even immersed in such wild splendor I can't avoid remembering how when we graduated high school, Ava had gone to a prestigious college and I had gone to work. She graduated several years later as a veterinarian; I had joined the Navy. She worked for several years as a vet around the rural farmland we grew up in before moving to Los Angeles and beginning a very lucrative practice.

Ava had a very visible office in just the right part of town to keep a client base of Hollywood's top power broker's pets healthy and well. I found it almost ridiculous, although I'd never admit it, that she had on her staff not only the finest veterinarians, but also a pet masseuse and an animal psychologist. Though lost on me, it had made her incredibly wealthy. The gap between our lifestyles was always a silent and negative presence.

We had met again, after years apart, over a simple friend request on a social networking site. Her first words to me knocked the wind right out of my lungs. I will never forget instantly making a commitment to myself to be a positive change in her life as I read, "I wake up every morning wanting to scream into my pillow."

She was ensnared in a loveless marriage with a cold and emotionless narcissist. A man who held her as a possession, used their children as psychological leverage, and consumed both her fine skills and the wages they garnered. All the while this man moved seamlessly from one distracting tryst to the next without remorse.

Exasperating the inherent difficulty built into this newly rediscovered love was my own career. I'd been in the Navy for seventeen years when we met again, a Senior Chief running an inspection team on forward deployed ships. The job forced an almost unmanageable travel schedule, and an incredibly unhealthy lifestyle of airports and hotel rooms.

Gone for weeks at a time, I was less than the single father I desired to be. My two daughters and I had lost their mother, my wife, to the recklessness of a drunk driver almost ten years earlier. Forced between being a single father and finishing the career to get the benefits of my pension, I had opted to send my two daughters away to a boarding school in Vermont.

Any one of these factors weighing on a relationship is a justifiable hardship to overcome. All of these combined obstacles

formed what I came to refer to only as "the static." Strung out
between constantly trying to be there to pay appropriate attention
to my job, my children, and my relationship, I'd grown to perform
each task with only the minimal investment of energy required to
keep it going; each had suffered from my neglect.

It strikes me as unbelievable to this day that we had not recognized love at first sight in our youth. In retrospect I believe my
innocent, and naïve, mind had simply assumed this was how all
relationships would be. I swore to myself not to repeat this foolish assumption and, upon beginning the relationship that lasted
for the next five years, I always carried the knowledge that I would
never love any other again.

As I walk my mind takes a stroll of its own, carrying me back
to a happier time. We had walked, hand in hand, down the board-
walk as the moon rivaled the streetlights overhead. On a playful
whim we had decided to ride the rollercoaster that stood before
us. The attendant spoke, of what I can't recall, but we all laughed
together. Then he had opened the gate as a waiter might open a
rare bottle of wine...deliberately.

She was sitting on my lap as I held her in my arms, seated
together in a metal car best described as vintage. The ride had
begun, but somewhere along the way it seemed to leave the bindings of the rails that held it. Off we sailed entwined together as if
in a spell, transcending time and space, the only two people in the
world, if only for that one brief minute.

A storm, some talking-head had named "super", tore that
magical place down, driving it into the sea. In my sleep, however,
that old wooden coaster still stands. In the ether world of dreams,
the smell of her hair still intoxicates me. Her body against mine
thrills me more than the twisting turns of any amusement park's
ride. When I wake I am always fully aroused, then my arms close

around nothing but memories; her absence is as solid as the darkness surrounding me.

I have no doubt that had we been reunited in a way deserving of the love we'd always shared, ours would've been a story penned by hand, in a leather-bound binding, emblazoned with gold filigree. Instead, we stepped into the love of a lifetime against seemingly insurmountable odds. We were to launch directly into the highest places love can lift a human soul, only to have the weight of the world pull us back down to Earth.

On the trail ahead of me is a small stream, a free rock flow that pools at its bends. The water is gin clear. The sound of the water being pulled along its route by gravity fills the air. It would certainly hold tiny brook trout, waiting like little green lions for anything alive that dared move through their fragile microcosmic world.

I take a broad step over a narrower section onto a large stone and push forward to the opposite bank. The traction of my boot is instantly lost. I feel a wave of nausea as my foot turns under the fulcrum of my ankle, and connective tissues pass their tolerances and part. I fall to the far bank in a heap.

Immediately I slide out of my pack and bend forward to get the boot off of my trembling foot knowing the swelling will be quick in arriving. Small fissures of blood have already appeared under my skin on the inside of my ankle. I cup my heel in my palm and feel it move as rockets of pain launch toward my brain.

I push my badly sprained ankle into the icy stream, cursing myself for my loss of awareness and the severity of my position. I'd learned years ago, at an arctic survival camp in Alaska, that the first rule of seeing your way through a life-or-death situation is recognizing when you are in one.

I am only 10 miles from the small town of Twin Mountain. I have two choices – to travel a trail to my east following the Zealand River, or to backtrack and follow the Little River north. Ten miles will take me days if I can't stabilize this foot. The nights are dropping well below the threshold of hypothermia. Pain will degrade my endurance, and I can't afford any more mistakes.

A cold sweat has broken across my head and shoulders, and my heart beats like the grouse's wings. I have to cut through the fog of the mind-numbing pain and focus. I am an experienced operator; I've led others through chaos before. I'm not about to lose my bubble now.

# CHAPTER 2

It's like standing on the equator of Mercury. The pain of having my foot in… or out of… the icy flow of the high mountain stream is unbearable. I release the tensioning straps from around my rucksack and spill its contents onto the ground.

There's a small military surplus bag that I've resurrected to serve as a makeshift EMT kit. I push aside all of the other collected items and open the bag's zipper as I cradle the bundle on my lap. There is a baseball-sized sphere of duct tape, and I reach for my knife.

I open the blade with one hand and ease its serrated edge deeply into the ball until I feel it hit resistance. I am hyper-vigilant not to push it into my palm, further exasperating my predicament. I carefully slice open the ball and pull out a sealed pill bottle. Several years ago I had surgery, and my dislike for strong narcotics led me to gutting out the pain rather than using the prescribed medication.

I'd decided to save the pills should I ever wind up breaking my femur above the scree line on a sheep hunt and needed to get back for help. I haven't done anything as traumatic as fracturing my leg, however, these pills will prove vital to clearing my head of pain so I can get myself out of the woods, both literally and figuratively.

I have no idea how much oxycodone to take, or if it is still be viable after all this time. I take two pills and drink them down with water from the stream. I figure I am now on a timer, and I need to stabilize my ankle and be mobile before the narcotic kicks in.

I roll my pants leg up as high as I can. Then I pull a SAM splint from the pack and unravel it, then fold it in half. I gingerly put my sock back on, although my wet skin makes it excruciating to do so.

I then bind the SAM splint tightly in place with an elastic bandage. I put my belongings back into my pack and include my discarded boot, incompetent as it was. I've compromised proper ankle support for a lower-cut, lighter-weight choice. Using a tree as a buddy I push up onto my feet and feel a wave of nausea again as my blood flows down and fills my swelling foot.

This is going to be a major pain.

I make quick work of searching the nearby area for proper sized limbs, and using the remains of my duct tape, I craft a rough pair of crutches. I'm miserable as consider my two trail choices, and then I remember the lights behind the ridgeline I'd seen less than seven hours before.

I ferret the GPS out of its pouch and spark it to life. I zoom in on my current position and regard the contour lines between me and a saddle in the mountain to my north. The eastern side is too rocky, and that will not do on crutches. If I go straight north, I can follow a large drainage that mellows the grade of the elevation changes. After plotting out some waypoints as references, I'll have less than one and a half miles to travel.

I can plainly see there is no town there. There were lights, though, and only people can create lights on that scale. Perhaps a film crew is making a movie, or some survival series is recreating a scene for reality television. Either way it makes no difference to me. I need help, and I need it now. So I off I go.

The night's previous frost has melted, and tiny drops of water hang from every turning leaf. I walk several times through small hammocks of blueberries. I do not know if opiates give you the munchies, but these blueberries are amazing. Is this why wild-eyed addicts get stuck in ventilation ducts trying to obtain midnight access to the pharmacy?

I'm getting through the woods much easier than I had dared to hope. The ground is a deep loam of slowly rotting deadfall and leaves, covered in a lush mat of moss that has bright British Soldiers standing their proud post in the midday's sun. I stop and pull aside the moss and carve out a rich handful with the blade of my palm. Tiny grains of sand fill the soil in an even blend. I reflect on how this would buffer the streams PH below me, all the while providing the mineral base for insects to develop themselves. These same insects will rise to the surface to test their wings, only to be ambushed by the bright flashes of the brook trout patrolling from beneath.

What a perfect cycle it all is. Hours earlier I'd focused on the tiny world the little trout were trapped in, and hadn't felt the connectivity between them and the dirt in my hand.

I look up through the filtering limbs of an old cedar standing above me. It gives shelter; it hosts life for the birds to feed on, and those birds and this tree will lie still one day and feed the dirt I stand on. Earth itself will flow down, pushed by the thaws of annual snows and the rains in between them to the trout, through the trout to the sea, then back to the hill as some later season's snow.

I suspect I may become an oxycodone addict.

I've come to the crest of the ridge in less than an hour. I anticipate having to scout for some time to determine the source of the lights I saw the night before. The search would be prove unnecessary; as I look at the scene before me I feel my head slowly tilt to the side as I subconsciously assume what I have always called, "the stupid dog look."

# CHAPTER 3

I had once been the coxswain of a small boat launched from a carrier when an F/A-18 had gone missing from the radarscope somewhere off the coast of someplace. The ELT had immediately gone audible, and using a deceptively simple handheld direction finder, we followed the warbling cry broadcasting out at 2182kHz to its source with no problem.

An aircraft looks so large, even a small fighter, when standing beside it. They are, however, ingeniously engineered from almost nothing with each piece giving support to the other. Once this cohesion is broken, they come apart like a house of cards built on a train track. We'd found no physical piece of the life lost that day except for a patch of green fabric. It was from a flight suit and, ironically, about the size of a card.

The surface chop where the plane had impacted was squelched flat by the large stain of JP-5 on the water. There was no piece of anything larger than a fragment of laminated carbon fiber, and it was smaller than the lid of a cooler. Most of what was left was filtering out of sight below and falling through the clear blue world of inner space. What I saw before me was nothing like that.

It's obviously a jumbo jet… an airliner of bright white and blue that has fallen from the sky. Its debris is scattered everywhere. As I said, I was trained and conditioned to survey scenes of crisis, and what strikes me is how literal my first impression is. This aircraft did not crash into a mountain; it fell from the sky.

There are no trees broken, no earth carved out by the plowing demise of a struggling pilot. Though hung with insulation, and paper, and clothing from luggage, all of the trees surrounding this wreck are unbroken. It's as if the plane simply dropped to the ground.

My own personal crisis is suddenly a moot point. There are bound to be survivors, even if only barely alive after hours in the elements. I clench down on my own teeth and begin making my awkward way to the site as quickly as possible. As I struggle along I reach again for my GPS, as I want to document the timeline of rescue efforts for those who will want to rebuild this event. The screen powers on but remains blank. The loss of satellite icon is blinking on and off at the top of the display.

The wind has been steadily coming from the south for the past few days, so it doesn't surprise me that I haven't smelled the fuel that is flowing from the hulking metal corpse. Apparently, when the plane crashed down, there weren't any ready sources of ignition for an explosion. There's not even a small secondary fire within sight. There is just four hundred tons of silent destruction lying in the valley between proud mountain peaks as if dropped by a giant child who has moved on to play with another toy.

I brace myself for the carnage of broken people's lost lives, and the ripped flesh and torn limbs I'll certainly encounter. As I round the starboard wing, I look inside of the crushed fuselage. There are tons of personal effects, baggage from overhead bins mixed with unnaturally folded seats, and clothing is everywhere.

But there are no people.

I back away, my mind doing random algebra... it must still be no later than eleven o'clock at the latest. This plane is obviously what'd awakened me in the night, just moments after three a.m. Where the hell are the helicopters? Why hasn't anyone arrived here yet? Why isn't the hungry carrion crow of the media circling overhead for the big scoop? Where's the media? Certainly you don't just lose a 747 from your stable and not bother to go out into the night looking for it!

I wait and ponder this for what seems like an eternity. Finally, I decide to make my way to the belly of the bird to see if there's anything there that can help me. I'll prepare myself better for back country travel, now without a GPS, and make my way northwest toward the town of Twin Mountain. I figure it to be no more than seven miles, and if I get too turned around, my route is framed on both sides by rivers. I'll eventually vector my way to help solve this conundrum, hopefully before dark.

I find some form of a maintenance box—a large molded plastic case full of costly tools, primarily meant for doing repairs to electronics. There are also some specialty tools for making emergency splices in hydraulic lines. In the bottom of this box, however, is something I know well. Two rolls of syntho-glass, a product that unwinds like tape that, when wetted with warm water, synthesizes into hardened fiberglass. Brilliant!

I pull my unfaithful boot out of my pack and snap open the blade from my hip. I make short work of sawing off the sole with the intention of building a walking cast right here on the spot. I empty my bottle into my gas stove's cooking chamber to warm the water I will require.

Then I take a large roll of gauze tape from my EMT kit and begin to unwind the rough splint. My ankle is bruised, yet the narcotics have been wonderful at taking the edge off the pain. Again I cup my heel gently in my hand and, despite the electric shocks that roll up my calf, I apply some solid torque to my ankle to take the temperature again of this injury.

Perhaps it's just my imagination… or the drugs… but it feels considerably more solid than before. Perhaps I've been a bit hasty in my initial assessment, and I'll only be laid up for a few weeks.

I wrap my foot heavily in gauze over my naked foot and shin. I wet the first roll of glass tape and wind it snuggly around my lower leg. I then place the cupped heel of my hiking boot onto my foot and wrap another layer of glass tape around the front of my toes, over the bridge of my foot and around the bottom, then finish the job with a couple of turns around the heel again. I use steady pressure from my hands to force out the air between the layers and feel as it begins to grow hotter as the fiberglass vulcanizes into one form.

I lie back onto my pack and scan the sky for any sign of any rescue craft on the horizon. There is no easy way out I see coming, so twenty minutes later I struggle onto my feet. My improvised cast proves steady, and the foot holds weight with minimal complaint.

I make my way toward the cockpit, where the locked safety door is torn from its hinges. Inside it I see, mixed in with the collection of paperwork, fallen wiring, and a pancaked cup of coffee, enough black pants and white shirts for three people and three pilot's combination covers.

I know it's a huge mistake. Never leave the scene in a wilderness emergency. Repeat that as necessary. *Never leave the scene*! But all of the rules are off of the table. The mechanics of simple physics, the binding on the book of reality had been fractured. And

I set off through unbroken wilderness on a half-assed cast and a head full of opiates; with a knife, a lighter, and a tent for insurance.

What could go wrong?

This is foolish; I feel uncertain and filled with doom. I can't shake the feeling that a film crew is hiding behind every tree with their hands clamped over their mouths, suppressing their laughter. America must be eating microwaved chicken tenders, washing them down with a soda, and laughing at me from their couches. I just know this has to be one big joke at my expense.

# Chapter 4

**B**reaking trail and heading through these north woods is far easier than I'd feared. I've grown accustomed to the thick density of the species that comprise the Southern woodland. In the South, the growth of any variety of brambles and briars fight their slow motion battle for the sun's energy, thus creating far more resistance for a man to break through than here. Holly trees and hemlocks grow wide apart to form the first canopy overhead. Spaced more distantly still, tall pines and spruces, aromatic cedars, and ancient maples tower together to form the second lush canopy.

The walk is almost pleasant, despite the fact that my head feels like a whirling hall of knives. I lean against the alabaster base of a birch tree and drink deeply from the collapsible water bottle I carry. In front of me the vertical lines of the tree trunks intersect with the horizontal lines of their limbs, and I see a brief vision of a weaver's masterpiece; a woodpecker and barking squirrels chimed a warning of my presence, but seem only to add to the living tapestry. It is the strangest day of my life. I feel terrified of something unknown, yet, simultaneously, lulled peacefully by everything that I see.

I come across a two-track road in the woods. It's a simple vehicle path, one that would perhaps take someone to their hunting camp. It led the right direction, and keeping the sun always behind my right shoulder, I continue on north.

A beaver has impounded a small stream, running parallel to the road. In the headwater of this small pond I see what appears to be a chain-link gate. I scan my surroundings quickly. Then I walk to the trap and spring it with a large limb the beaver provided thoughtfully for just this task. It snaps shut with deceiving force, and the limb is wrenched from my grasp and roughly broken.

Less than a half-mile further up the road, I see a small pickup truck pulled off to the side and into the trees. I begin yelling in earnest to get the attention of its owner. As I walk past the truck I see a bed full of fast food bags, empty beer cans, and a large brush-stroke of blood across the open tailgate. Through the driver's window I see an old bolt-action rifle nested between the seats. There's a handheld spotlight plugged into the cigarette lighter. A beer can rides proudly in the cup holder.

In a small clearing not fifty feet away, a deer is hanging by its feet from the limb of a tall maple. Its ankles have been impaled by a rough gambrel made from bent reinforcement bar; its organs hang out, still attached to the body. On the ground is a thick bladed knife.

On the spot now made profane by a poached young doe is a complete set of clothing, including a snap-back hat reading, "the buck stops here", and a pair of worn work boots with socks still inside them. All of these clothes are completely covered with ash.

My mind is reeling at full force now. It's as if reality has just crested the top of a slow climb up the tracks, and my intellect holds its hands over its head and screams as the ride shoots straight down on greased rails.

There are only three viable options I can arrange into a thought. Either a poacher has gone whiskey drunk into the night naked and insane, I have simply slid off the rails in my own mind and am in the middle of a psychotic episode, or, something truly awful is afoot and I am slowly discovering the rules regarding its occurrence.

I am babbling and trying to steady my hands as I climb into the truck and turn the engine over. I shove the shifter into first gear and begin driving to the closest town to figure out what is happening. Maybe a brief stay in a nice room with a view is in order?

I come hurling off the unpaved two- track and take a hard left across a narrow highway. I barrel directly into the parking lot of what's obviously a Mom and Pop hardware store. I egress the pickup still running behind me with absolute abandonment, and trip onto the front porch.

Looking around, I see there's actually still a payphone out front, and a neat face cord of hardwood is stacked over to my right. These would be good, rugged people capable of calming my unraveling mind with a cup of "honest" coffee. Perhaps they can get me a local constable who will take me to get proper medical attention, as I listen to his radio telling of the rescue of the doomed flight.

I climb back to my feet and reach for the doorknob. It is locked. I bang on the door yelling to get anyone's attention, seeing that the upstairs appears to be a residence. I walk over to the payphone… no signal. I bang and yell some more, and then reach over to the woodpile and insert one of the split pieces of firewood through a windowpane.

In a moment of clarity, I remove the large military knife from my waist and set it down; no need to justify being deflated by a shotgun blast as I open the door by brandishing a perceivable weapon. I reach through the broken window and turn the handle of a simple deadbolt and open the door.

# Chapter 5

Inside the hardware store is complete silence. The old clock on the wall reads 12:21 p.m. An antique cash register sits on a plywood counter that has any number of cards and fliers taped and pinned to it. On the wall a small sign says, "Paying with credit is like fishing without bait. Neither will work around here." I see a door in the rear of the store that I imagine leads upstairs to either apartments, or where the proprietor lived. Again I yell out but receive no reply.

I open the door to the rear; it leads a bead-boarded hallway with a flight of stairs. On the floor by my feet is a disturbingly large dog bowl. I decide to make a lot of noise so as not to disturb a sleeping dog. Not that walking up hardwood stairs with three pounds of fiberglass hardened around one's foot is exactly the preferred entry method of a cat burglar. Better safe than sorry.

I yell out once more before heading upstairs.

The first door opens into a humble kitchen with a round dining table. The living room is fitted with a tired old couch with a handmade red, white, and blue quilt draped over it. On the coffee table sits a dirty plate, a fork, and a small glass with what appears to be juice in the bottom. I turn the corner toward the bedroom;

there is no door on the hinge. There, lying on the bed is the shadow of a person. I walk over, confused.

The person was there, but not in the flesh. It's as if very fine clippings of thin hair, snowflakes of dust, and tiny filaments of fiber have been deposited painstakingly. Perhaps by an old monk painting a mandala. Each layer of dust has collected gently onto the ones below as if three dimensionally printed into the replication of an old man. The parts of his being, which had been under the heavy blankets, have collapsed.

There is no apprehension, no fear, there is no malice in the air at all and the scene before me feels rather beautiful in a macabre sort of way. Inside, however, I feel large gears of machinery beginning to spin as a thought I've purposefully withheld becomes unavoidable. I've no real idea what it means; the plane, the clothes, the deer hunter, the ashes of the shopkeeper. But, I know two things. I know my two daughters, and even as the idea comes rising up from the ether of my thoughts the word "no" comes out of my mouth so violently it scares me.

I run down the stairs two at a time, through the store, grabbing a paper almanac from a rack beside the counter as I pass. I sit for a moment in the truck and try to focus. The word "no" is chugging out of my mouth like the blow off of pressure from a locomotive's exhaust ports. I fumble with the almanac and see my route as a straight shot of less than 70 miles from this location to my daughters' school.

I slam the gearshift home and throttle out onto the road headed west. In less than two miles I spot a state patrol car off to the side of the road. I skid to a stop with my bumper coming to rest against a section of guardrail. Getting out of the truck, I head directly to the cruiser. Looking in the window, I can see the keys still hanging in the ignition. I walk around to the back of the car and there, on the ground, is a brown uniform stacked atop a pair of heavy military boots. In the middle of the pile is a dark blue ballistic vest, and all throughout there's a heavy caking of gray ashes.

I open the door to the cruiser and start the engine. Then I shut it off, pull the keys, and walk around and open the trunk. I pull out the small-framed assault rifle from its cradle and find five thirty-round magazines in a small bag beside it. I pull the charging handle to the rear, lock the bolt back, look into the chamber, and insert a magazine.

I slap the side of the receiver around the bolt release, and a live round is sent into the chamber. A quick turn of the firing selector tells me the rifle is fully automatic. I ensure it's on safe, and then I climb back into the cruiser and pull out in a hail of tire smoke headed west. Seventy miles to the school has just become a far shorter distance.

As I shoot down the highway, I fumble through every communications device in the vehicle. The radio will only produce static. The onboard computer boots up, but a login password immediately stymies me. The cop's cellphone sits on the center console but has no signal. It still works though... applications will open, pictures will display. But no reception.

About halfway to the school, shortly after passing into Vermont, I skirt a larger town and see a sign for a hospital. I will again revisit the makeshift cast on my foot as it's nagging me constantly. I pull of the exit and into the emergency room entryway.

I'm quickly forming the rules around myself of what is happening. At three o'clock in the morning, some event transpired that reduced all the people I've come across into a powder of ash and dust. For whatever reason, I have not been affected. It's a time where apocalyptic stories of every type are inundating popular culture... Zombie movies, alien invasions, and strange medical experiments gone virally wrong. I've yet to subscribe to a theory of my own. The military M-4 carbine does, however, find its way over my shoulder as I enter the hospital.

With the exception of a few cars in the median, and an occasional tractor-trailer in the trees, the road here has been pretty barren. The emergency room is little different. There are remnants of orderlies, nurses, and doctors. There is a bed here and there with a hospital issued gown covering dust and/ or ashes. Otherwise the place is completely empty. Nothing beeps; no PA announces the need for a doctor, or the arrival of an ambulance.

I quickly find what I am looking for, and close my eyes at my own stupidity. There's no power in the receptacles. There's no way to use this saw to remove the cast. Plan "B" immediately forms in my mind, and I set off back to the patrol car after liberating a few candy bars from the vending machine. This is actually rather fun in a macho and cliché sort of way.

I pull out of the hospital parking lot, going over the curb to avoid a garbage truck, which just sits there waiting for employment. I drive back to the highway overpass I'd just come from having seen a large home improvement store by the highway. In minutes I'm again breaking and entering as I help a stray shopping cart, designed to carry stacked lumber, to go through the locked sliding glass doors of the entrance.

I don't even need a plan. I simply know what to do in these places. I've always enjoyed a childlike love of hardware and building stores. I grab a five gallon bucket, walk straight to plumbing, cut off 8 feet of thin, clear plastic tubing, and return to the parking lot to siphon some gasoline from any car in the lot other than mine.

Coming back into the store with half a bucket of gasoline, I walk by the outdoor patio furniture and leave the fuel on a display gas grille. I spot the lawn mowers and walk down that aisle; in the next aisle I see what I need. I pull open the box, rip some of the ridiculous over-packing aside, and remove a sprayed in foam-shipping block revealing a small portable gas generator.

I carry the generator, much like a seventies roller-skater might've hefted along a boom box, to the front section of the store. There's a colorful display of everything from welders to book shelves filled with paperback volumes on "Idiot's Guide to the Deck," and "Carpentry Accounting for Material Thickness." I grab a reciprocating saw and a pack of short, fine blades designed for cutting tile. At least when I cut myself, it being factored into my best estimate, it will not be a jaggedly edged cut.

I drop these items into a bright orange grocery cart and push them over to the canvas gazebo that will be my M.A.S.H. tent. I marvel at this mauve gazebo and try to imagine what Sultan of Suburbia would have use for this structure erected on their property. I shove the swinging couch that is inside of the tent out among the riding mowers and drag a nearby picnic table inside. I'm not certain why I feel the need for doing this in a tent. Even as I smile at the ludicrous gesture I'm creating I carry on, undeterred.

I put the generator on the table and unscrew the fuel cap. Spilling less than expected I cap it back off, placing the open bucket of gasoline onto the polished cement floor and pushing it several extra feet away. I prime the carburetor, and close the simple butterfly choke. Still not certain of what I'm in the middle of, I scan the nearby store for movement – of zombies, aliens, and viruses alike. Satisfied the sound won't mask an approaching brain eater, I put the M-4 on the table and pull the start cord on the generator.

One pull and it's chugging along. The generator has been kept warm, so I simply open the choke and it hums straight to operating speed. I install a blade into the saw and plug in the cord.

Nothing.

I reach over and reset the breaker on the receptacle, and we have ignition. I place the blade into the top of the cast between the fiberglass and the gauze and let it start to eat some material.

I cut very slowly all the while allowing the saw to run at maximum speed. This allows me to control the depth the blade inside the confines of the cast. As I get near to my toes I put the saw down and massage the cast open until it parts neatly in half. If I were a betting man, which I am, I would have lost five dollars on my not having at least three solid and painful new tears in my skin.

As it is, the gauze comes off cleanly, and I look at my destroyed heel. There's no bruising at all. I look at my foot as if waiting for it to initiate a conversation. I attempt some simple movements. My ankle is sore, as if hit by a wildly bouncing baseball in the infield, but I can walk on it.

I sit down and take a brief inventory of my situation. I'd been awakened in the middle of the night all giddy and dreamy-eyed as a jet full of dust people had fallen out of the sky miles away. I tore my ankle to shreds and was afraid of being stranded in the woods to die, but it healed in a few hours. I am now running across state lines in a stolen police cruiser and brandishing a Title-II firearm.

Somehow, it all seems reasonable.

Not certain what else to do, I decide to find a new pair of shoes. There's nothing like a little retail therapy to help ease angst from frayed nerves. I take off my one remaining boot so at least as I walk out the front door I'm not pitching back and forth like a demented fool. Maybe the first police officer to yell "freeze!"

won't then yell, "Hey, who did that?" as some rookie cop puts a bullet into my head. I find the parking lot still empty.

Back on the highway after a brief stop at a shoe store, and less than twenty minutes of hard driving later, I apply the brake pedal with a wonderfully overpriced leather boot. I coast across the bridge onto the grounds of the Boarding Academy where my daughters have gone these last few years. I'm certain they are fine. I knew it in my heart they're scared and waiting in their rooms. Or, perhaps the headmaster has assembled all of the students into the auditorium and they are devising a plan for dealing with this event.

I enter the main hall of the school through the front doors. These doors have always made me think of the Methodist church I attended with my family when we were once again living as a unit after a major car accident. My young friends and I would go off fishing, or playing hockey, then walk right into the unlocked church and brew a pot of coffee. We were maybe twelve, thirteen at the oldest, and we sat in the chapel in the pews to warm ourselves, talking and laughing.

We'd clean up the mess, rearrange the drying pieces of the large percolator as we found them, and place our cups into the dishwasher for someone else's future load to clean. There was wine in the cupboards, but we were never tempted. There were large golden-colored crosses, and a rather impressive wooden relief of Jesus Christ's crucifixion. The group of kids I ran with would never have thought to vandalize a thing.

Sure, we'd hop coal trains and ride them for miles just to get to new locations to fish for Smallmouth Bass. And we'd have older brothers, and sisters, buy us tobacco and pilfer the occasional *Playboy*. But we were good kids in the end, and life back then afforded good kids a lot more room to stray than the world we built as adults.

The doors of the school, too, were always open. It was a school that taught us that hard work is just a part of life. It was a school where trust was assumed, faith was given, and betrayal was dealt with as the true failure it was. I enter the main hall and head to the stairs into the girls' dormitory rooms.

I don't yell this time. The silence is doing the yelling, and my heart is frozen as I run up the stairs. All of the dorm room doors are adorned with paper signs demanding privacy and brightly-painted cards bearing the occupant's name. They are also all closed. I come to my youngest daughter's room, and with my head on the door, I turn the handle.

It's very dark in here, despite the bright sunshine outside. She's a very light sleeper and is very crafty when it comes to getting those last minutes sleep undisturbed by the morning sun. Lying there in her bed is my little girl's shadow. Her body is collapsed under the burden of comforters and blankets. But her beautiful face is preserved like a bust made of the lightest of keepings; fibrous windings of the minutest details collect to create her image as beautiful as she's ever been.

I hear my own breath through my nose, and feel the push of tears welling through my eyes. I give in to it and begin to simply bawl. I cry openly. I cry for my little girl, gone from me, and I cry for her not ever hearing one last time, "I love you too."

I walk down the hall to my eldest daughter's room and walk right in as if I've already surrendered to the fact she, too, will be gone. I kneel by her bed and softly say hello to the image of my little girl reproduced lying before me. I put my face close to hers. The details are so powerful; I can see her eyelashes and the thin smile on her lips. She'd gone into this state smiling.

Through the open blinds in the window, a single ray of sun cuts through the room and alights onto her head. The beam seems to part straight through the layers of downy hair, fragments of bright thread, and hollow balls of white lint. Through the shell of her I can see the light playing within. The movement of the sun so many miles away is enough to spark bright flashes of a color with no name, a color of life, of love, of magic. Somehow through my sobbing I manage to say, "You always were such a brilliant girl. Then I add, "…Both of you," as I rise to my feet then walk back down the stairs to the main floor.

I walk down the hall to the art room and find a large document tube. I reach for my knife and then remember I've left it on the porch of the store in my haste. Rather than cutting the tube in half, I decide to simply grab two of them. They appear to be used chart tubes. Plastic caps fitting neatly into their ends will hold their contents safely inside.

I take them back upstairs and return to one room, then the other, painstakingly gathering every part of my children and storing them in unmarked cardboard tubes. When I get to my second child, I see a small necklace on her chest. It's a heart with a diamond that I'd given her some years earlier. I reach out to gently remove it, but the illusion is broken and the image collapses like a building falling flatly under its own weight.

I walk out to the police cruiser and put the two tubes of my daughters into the passenger seat. Then I reach over, and without thought, I buckle them in… always wanting only to protect them.

# CHAPTER 6

I stop at the small barn on the property of the school. The faculty and students worked together to maintain a well-running little pocket farm as part of the curriculum. All of the vegetables grown augmented the kid's diets. The animals were tended to by the children in order to teach the solid values of simple living. This included the annual harvesting of the chickens with the kids as participants.

The barn is still closed from the previous night. I decide that I should do my best to liberate the animals. The horses will die in the coming winter without people to tend to them. It just seems cruel somehow to leave them locked inside to starve to death.

I walk straight up to the rolling door, open the latch, and pull it open along its track. The sun floods the inside with warm colors of gray and brown. The smells in here are old smells, familiar and calm... the tack room, saddle soap, and leather.

I walk over to where the stalls are lined down a long wide hall. They are all empty. There's a lead clipped to a pad eye at the front of each stall. Each lead is in turn clipped to a bridle that simply sits on a freshly mucked bedding of clean straw.

A quick round of the farmyard confirms a growing theory for a yet another new rule. Animals have been spared from this destructive event. There are still woods full of birds and deer, and I've seen signs of animals in abundance along the trail. But all of mankind is apparently gone, and so, too, are mankind's animals.

I drive from the school into the town center, as I need a tank of gasoline. I have a suspicion that the hassle of siphoning and then pouring the gallons of fuel I require shall prove to be a bore, so instead I'll simply get a new vehicle. Perhaps I'll be trading in one slightly used New Hampshire State Police interceptor for something more fitting of my mood— the rifle I'll be holding onto.

I park the cruiser right in the middle of the road. Truth be told, I'd love nothing more than to get a ticket. I don't. I walk steadily over to an outdoor sports retailer who's earned more than a few hard-earned dollars from me over the last few years, feeling nothing more than a cold flame in my chest. I swing the carbine off of my shoulder and center the doorknob in the ghost ring of the rifle's rear sight.

I'd only just begun to unleash a stream of anguish upon the locked door when the rifle stops on the second shot. It's not fully automatic after all—it's a three round burst. Funny thing to get angry about, but being robbed of the release I desire pisses me off to no end.

I thumb the selector switch straight up into semiautomatic and bring the weapon down, parallel to the ground. I pop the sling loose from the rifle's stock, and as it hangs from the front, I step on it with my boot's toe. This will arrest the rise of the muzzle. I release the last 28 rounds as quickly, and thoughtlessly, as hand and machine can work together.

One true advantage of shooting from the hip is that without a gun in your face you can thoroughly enjoy the freestyle dance of destruction in its full visual glory. The one true disadvantage is that you cannot hit a damned thing. The door stands there in bold defiance; the lock remains completely unscathed.

I walk over as though everything is fine. "Nothing to see here", the fat beat cop would say. "Move along."

I swiftly kick the open the front door, like any sane crazy-man would've done in the first place. Immediately inside is a brand new, very much my style, black and gray hard-shell jacket. It's easily worth eight hundred dollars, had I not just completed it with at least three visible holes.

There reaches a point where things officially get as bad as they can get, and one just has to laugh. I don't laugh. I have absolutely no inclination to laugh. I do notice at approximately this point, however, that I doubt things can get much worse.

I strip completely naked and walk downstairs to the camping supplies. I grab a pack of personal wipes and do a quick house-keeping of the nether regions. I open up plastic bags full of over-priced polypropylene base layer thermals and dress into them.

I find a solid pair of adventure pants that are a cross between a farmer and military tactical. Judging by their name, apparently, that's who builds boats. I find a tight-fitting quarter-zip top and put a very nice gray wool sweater on over it.

I walk back up the stairs, around the broken glass on the floor, to the shoes. I pull on a pair of synthetic wool socks, and find a pair of mountaineering boots that catch my eye. Ducking into that mysterious place the "shoe dude" normally would go to grab my boots, I find my size. I then fumble the laces into a working order and put them on my feet. A pair of top-end snow bibs, a tightly quilted down jacket, and the exact hard-shelled coat I eyeballed at the entrance, are pulled off of their racks as I quickly outfit myself. I look as though I'm either about to attempt to climb K2, or to take on the world.

On my way out the door I grab a hat that seems appropriate and some gauntlet styled gloves. Cursing my less-than-smooth getaway, I walk back in to find a good pair of contact layer gloves to wear beneath the gauntlets. Then I head back into the cruiser to drive around the world's biggest used car lot looking for the next good deal.

I drive without purpose through the side streets of this small city. A steady snow has begun to fall. It's the little flaked kind of snow that accumulates deceptively quickly, and the police cruiser is proving less and less up to the task as I continue through a small sub-development.

I stop the car and back up a few feet, rolling down the window for a better view. From the hillside, I can see down into the city's motor pool. There, in the middle of the lot, sits a green emergency vehicle.

Through the growing wind of the building snow squall I can hear it calling to me. I may be in my forties and supposed to be done with toys. I may be having the worst day anyone has had since the advent of fire, but I simply can't resist. There are rules I'm still discovering about this mysterious phenomenon… everything has clearly changed. But one thing has not: boys like their toys.

I fishtail my way through the silent streets, and I can't help feeling the loss. I already long for the people, the kids playing around the yards of these empty houses. I miss my dreams of a home, of a place I feel safe. I can't help but remember the promises made in times that'd seemed so real. I remember believing once that I had something nobody else could know. It was real to me; it had imprinted onto my soul. I feel the strong ache of that promise being broken. It's all gone now, and the pull on me is breaking my heart evermore.

I drive through the chain-link fence that surrounds the city's collection of snowplows, emergency vehicles, and a few pedestrian looking sedans with tax exempt tags on their bumpers. I pull up beside a huge and relatively new Unimog, proudly emblazed with the seal of the state on its door, the word "EMERGENCY" is stenciled in reverse across its hood.

I climb into the cab and toss the rifle onto the passenger's side floor. I put my daughters tightly in the gap between the passenger's seat and the large center console. I turn the battery switch on, and by the light of the moon coming through the windshield I'm able to figure out the switches readily enough.

First the oil pump is primed, then the glow plugs cycle until a green start light illuminates on the dashboard. I push in the clutch, turn the starter switch on, and the steady explosions of compressed diesel in cold steel begin an uneven cadence as the truck comes back to life.

A hard snow is now falling outside. The windshield wipers clear my vision, as I roll out of the parking lot and onto the main street through town. I'm crying with no reservations as I work through the gears and come back onto the highway out of town. The large truck barrels down the snow covered road like a bull with wild high beams for eyes, terrified as it runs through the streets.

I have lost everything, and I am broken. I have no home, no family...

I had begun my hike furious at Ava for abandoning me. During the months of solitude that followed, I'd come to see it was my own ego, not her betrayal, that'd failed me after all.

I had found the resolve to finish the trail and head home to California. Once there I would write a heartfelt letter, to open myself fully and vulnerably to her. I had held onto the hope that she, too, would remember the love of a lifetime. I had faith that if I surrendered to the power of forgiveness, the power of love, what'd come to feel so wrong could be set right. And now, through some cruel twist of fate, it's all gone; gone to ashes and dust.

Through my tears, and the smears of the wipers, I see a hard curve ahead. Putting my foot to the firewall, I make no effort to shepherd this stampeding beast around the tight turn.

The large tires break from their beads, and the guardrail is flattened as if made of papier-mâché. I watch as the stars and moon spin up out of view, and the headlights illuminate trees growing violently larger. The seatbelt grows tight, and I watch as the windshield explodes toward me. On instinct, I reach over to shelter my daughters with my arm.

# CHAPTER 7

Away from the well-lit security of streets made safe for the nightly parades of debauchery in a city tailored for sin, an unfinished man requests no consent from a pretty young coed. Her mind is blurred and confused from an unfeeling pharmaceutical, unwittingly easing the wrong man's pain.

Hands dirty and callused by a lifetime of work have hammered the button of her nose into a flowing river of crimson. The dark stain of her blood wicks down through her fashionably inadequate shirt. Useless sobs through freshly loosened teeth are bleating out into an uncaring night. Her eyebrow splits open against the handle of an overflowing trashcan as he brutally tries to finish himself. She heaps into the rain soaked ground and finds herself surprisingly reflective of the small town she was dying her entire life to leave.

⋏

I am kicking and swinging wildly at unseen assailants. My voice is leaving me like that of a raccoon with its broken hand in a steel trap. I can feel the horror of being jailed in the mind of a young girl, as her fairytales are brutally smashed against rocks as a bear might kill a fish trapped in a shallow pool.

I can also feel the fury of pain, a mind numbed by a fog of cheap liquor as his moral compass swings randomly, lost in the deviation of a self-imposed prison and filled with predators who feed off of the hopes and innocence of others.

Even as I realize I am, in fact, ripping my own hands across broken glass and kicking my bruised shins against steel and the levers of a sophisticated transfer case, I can feel the horror that was always a part of the world I'd once walked through so blindly.

Just as I'd not considered before the weight of the soil as the rain gently carried its way through the cycles of creation, I had not thought properly of my place in the same cycle. I'd ignored the weight of the creative wonder that we had so mutually neglected as we made ourselves the centers of our own delusional worlds. And now it was too little to see, and I'd seen it too late.

I collect the tubular bodies of my children, grab the carbine by the butt stock, and drag myself out through the hole where once a heavy door had been solidly hanging beside me. There are to be many new rules to learn, I can plainly see.

I would not have to awaken daily to revisit my own failings as in a movie I'd once watched. But I was not going to be able to simply cash out so easily, either. I can smell the rotten stench of spoiled rosemary and burnt oil; gear case oil has never sat well on my palette.

I climb weakly through the bases of small bushes, now dormant for the winter, using them as I leverage my way back up the steep frozen hillside. I'd just sledded down this sheer drop off, like an action figure placed into a toy truck and pushed off the front porch of a safe suburban home. When I get to the horizontal surface of the road, I pull my hood over my head and curl into a ball as the wind and the snow drive against me.

# CHAPTER 8

The indigenous people of this continent believed that the raven carries the souls of ancient Shamans. I have just enough native blood to occasionally feel more rooted to the earth than was considered normal by my peers. I've always wanted a pet raven. Perhaps it was childhood wonder that the birds could mimic words. Perhaps it's a throwback to a grandmother who steeped me in old Charles Addams books, and would read to me the writings of Poe.

Once while driving to school as a teenager, I'd seen an injured raven hoping across a snow covered cornfield. The corn had been cut, and the stalks protruded like skeletal elbows rising out of the ground. The raven's black form was sharply contrasted against this polarized scene.

I'd parked my car as closely as possible and chased a hopping and loudly complaining bird well over a hundred yards before I finally dove on him and caught him between gloved hands. It'd proceeded to apply its large and capable beak to me with great enthusiasm as I carried it to my car and loosely bound it into my jacket.

I returned home and placed it into a small pet carrier, I gave it some water and raw hamburger then set off back for school, now late, along with the two girls I picked up daily along the way. I bragged to everyone all day of how I would finally have my pet raven. I couldn't wait to get home.

During the day my mother had seen the raven in her laundry room, and a lifelong fascination with lice, or mites, or cooties of some flavor had motivated her to stick it outside. Once safely outside where it could not infest the home with what certainly was an infantry of parasites, it had slowly died of exposure. Buy the time I had arrived home from school, I was disturbed to discover what had become the family story of "the crowcicle."

Why I'm feeling reflective on my mere minutes-long adventure of owning such a pet becomes obvious as I lift my head through the snow. A large raven leaps back, startled, spreading his wings to make himself more imposing. As I rise to my feet shaking clean my layered clothing, it flies frantically between the guardrails and a low birch tree. It harangues me for scaring it so rudely; a large dropping sits nearby on the snow, which I accept as physical evidence of its complaint.

I say politely, "good morning, sir." It fills its chest and hackled guard feathers in a show of defiance. I laugh and say, "Or is that ma'am?" It lifts its head and makes a sound like a large drop of water falling deep into an underground pool. It flies off above me, and I watch it vanish into the limbs of a heavily laden pine.

I turn and begin walking toward the next town, which I know is some miles further through these steep mountains. Less than a quarter mile down the road I watch a rabbit freeze in place, thinking it unseen. I unsling the rifle from my shoulder and smoothly take it out with a high velocity round through the neck.

I pick my quarry up by its hind feet then walk back to the scene of my "accident" from the night before. I cup my hands around my mouth and look toward the opening where the raven has entered its roost. I make my best effort to reproduce the guttural tone the bird spat at me for insulting its obvious masculinity.

"Galoopt. Galoopt." I wave my arms and the rabbit like a fool dancing in the town square.

I throw the dead rabbit away from myself, but still in plain view on the road. I turn and walk about a hundred yards, then sit on the guardrail and fish an energy bar from my pocket. The bar is a prize I've garnered while no longer having to bother with the inconvenience of standing at the register and actually pay for what I need.

In very short order, just long enough to signal it was his idea all along, the raven spirals out of the tree like a falling Sopwith Camel. It lands deceptively lightly, despite its rapid decent squarely onto the sacrificed rabbit. It looks at me and caws a common call. I get to my feet and simply continue on my way.

In the middle of that afternoon, I reach the next small town. I break into a gas station and empty a few pull-topped cups of something alleging to be stew, and eat it cold with a plastic spoon from the coffee station. I walk back to the coolers and eye the wide display of crafted beers. Instead, I leave two empty water bottles on the ground and then exit and walk on. My pockets are, however, rather stuffed full of my favorite candy bars.

As the evening begins to settle in I enter a nearby home, which sits just off of the road. I light a fire in the living room and do not enter the bedrooms, nor do I examine the property. I simply sit on the floor with my back against the sofa, close my eyes, and absorb the heat from the fire.

A loud pop of sap boiling in the wood makes me open my eyes with a start. I look across the built-in shelving around the hearth, awash in a warm glow from the fire. I see a model boat, and a few books.

The ocean calls to you always, once you've lived at sea long enough to feel at home among the cresting of high waves and the dark mysteries beneath them. I rise and select a large reference book I recognize from my qualification phase as a Deck Watch Officer. I'd used this book as I was earning my certification to assume the responsibility of driving a large ship under my own authority.

No small part of this process is learning a secret language know only to a few, terms like variation, deviation, unequal prop thrust, and bank suction. I feed two thick logs into to fireplace and arrange them onto the hot coals with a tool placed handily in a large galvanized bucket filled with ashes.

I fan through the book, mainly looking at familiar pictures. And then I see it there on a page, and the significance is instantly recognized by my mind.

Righting Moment.

Righting Moment is the tendency for a ship to return to an even keel as two opposing forces strive toward a point of equilibrium.

One force is that of the center of the ship's gravity pushing down, the other is the force of buoyancy pushing up. Quite simply, it is like how a pendulum if left unassisted will always stop pointed directly downward. That is a simplification though, as there is no opposing force in constant contrast trying to hold the pendulum stuck to the ceiling.

A ship does, however, have a second force applying itself against its want to sit proudly on the skin of the sea. When the force of gravity prevails in this dynamic sparring match, if gravity is deemed the winner, a stricken ship will lie silently on the ocean's floor.

This is what has happened to the world around me. There are two forces always at work around us as we walked blindly through our existences. One is always seeking equilibrium. The other force is always pulling us further and further downward. The irony being this downward force was of our own creation all along.

The point had been reached where the weight of heaviness forcing down all at once had finally overcome the uplifting energy trying only to return to its own peaceful equilibrium. It becomes not an idea to me; it becomes knowledge, that at this moment the creator has simply removed the weight pushing downward. It does nothing to uncoil the spinning questions in my mind as to of why I am still here. It is simply giving me a name to focus my thoughts upon.

It is the Righting Moment

# CHAPTER 9

In the early hours of the morning, I look at the fire burning by my feet. It's now little more than just a cooling bed of coals. I push myself up onto the couch and lace on my boots. I collect my few belongings: my rifle, my daughters, my foul weather gear, and I simply walk out the door. I say, "Thank you," as I exit, and then I continue on down the same road as before.

There is a larger home a few short miles away. It was obviously built for someone more affluent from the cities to the east. The house sits on a high hill overlooking a small canyon with a steep walled river in its groin. I climb the stonewall next to the security gate and cross the front yard, right into their living room through an impressive picture window now in pieces under my boots. I walk through the home and into the kitchen. In the pantry I find several jars of baked beans, some pseudo-gourmet canned soups, and a bottle of nice Spanish red wine.

I collect these into the obligatory grocery bag hanging from a hook on the back of the door. All designer wives need to be seen carrying their groceries inside of such 'must have' shopping accessories. This one's emblazoned with the words, "We are all one world."

I need to use the restroom and feel no remorse for the fact there would be no water to flush with when I finish. I walk back the hall and into another room. I pause before a sight I take longer to process than I would have assumed of myself. There is a stainless steel sex toy of specific design lying in the middle of a pile of ashes, enough for at least two people.

This is a pretty obvious scene. What catches me off guard is that there are two jellyfish on the bed mixed in with the ashes. The stupid dog in me tilts his head as he processes this unlikely assembly of ingredients. The lights suddenly come back on in my mind. They are the silicone implants from a breast augmentation and have simply fallen onto the bed as their host was reduced instantly into ash.

I continue down the hall and find the large master bathroom. I use it, and as I leave, I notice an artfully composed picture of the couple that owned the home. On my way down the hall, back to the guest bedroom, I reach into the men's pants on the floor and pull out the wallet. The driver's license inside does not match the man photographed in the master bedroom. I look at the scene on the bed and mutter, "Ashes to ashes, we all fall down."

I proceed through the front of the house and enter the garage. I open the car's door, and the key is hanging neatly from the ignition switch on the dashboard. I reach up and pull the safety release from the electric garage door and open it manually.

I put everything I am carrying into its place beside me and back out onto the drive as a song comes onto the radio. It's a sad country western song, and it strikes me how out of place it is in the confines of this rosewood and leather interior. I head down the driveway, noticing an older Jeep partially hidden behind an outbuilding and figure it must belong to the interloper in the guest room. I continue down and through the gate.

I have nowhere in particular to go. I think of driving east and investigating the cities. But they will be choked full of debris no differently in their death than they were in their life. So I opt instead to simply follow the road before me. I drive over the Hudson River well north of the city. I continue south and west following no particular route.

At one point, on a major highway westbound into Pennsylvania, I'm forced off the highway by wreckage from a major collision. It seems that two trucks laden with fuel, or some commercial by-product of a sincerely insidious nature, had met their ends together on the bridge out of New Jersey. The explosion that followed rendered the bridge visibly unsafe from a good distance away, and I exit following the Delaware River south.

My stolen utility vehicle runs out of gas just as I enter Frenchtown, NJ. It is a quaint little burg; a cemetery, and small church mark it's center. An old and proud home has been converted into a bed and breakfast just around the corner from the downtown.

The streets off the town's Main Street are basically numbered one to ten. What starts as a desire to stay overnight in the B&B becomes an easy string of one day flowing into the next. I make a home of sorts in that place. I stay here almost five full months before spring arrives and fills my wings with the want to take flight.

# CHAPTER 10

I take deer and small game from the surrounding farmlands. At night I sit by the fireplace in the old converted home in a large leather chair. The library on the walls of the sitting room is surprisingly well stocked to my taste. An eclectic blend of books on biology and theology are randomly mixed to create a very desirable space from which I can try to settle into my place in this new world.

I've been spared both ashes and dust. The remnants of what was once my fellow mankind. I call them simply the "uppers" and "downers." I am no closer to figuring out *why* though. I make it my mission to try to decipher the clues I'm certainly overlooking. I first start where I think is most obvious, with the Bible.

I read the Bible front to back. I then read it front to back again. I find some useful things from the Old Testament. Mainly that, apparently, when God wants you to hang around for a while, he can arrange for a man to live far longer than I suspect I'd ever desire to exist. Second, I determine that the Old Testament is really more of an owner's manual for clean and healthy living in a world with neither antibiotics nor refrigeration, than that of the enlightened Holy Scripture I'd anticipated.

It is the New Testament that shakes me.  The words of Jesus Christ are printed in red.  It seems to me that while there is not a word to explain why I'm sitting here reading the Bible, the words of this man are truly worthy of the religion that has followed in his name.  He speaks one message.  His message is perfectly linear and never strays off point.  The man's point is simple:

Love.

Love is a word that I long to understand.  I sit one evening in the large leather chair.  I've built a spectacular fire and am almost too warm in its radiant heat while outside a storm of magnificent power is howling through the streets.  Thin clouds gallop by, quickly illuminated brightly against a black sky by the third full moon I've seen since the Righting Moment.

Inside I sit comfortably in my little unlocked cell, my legs crossed at the ankles, bare feet feeling pampered as they soak up the heat after a hard day of wearing snowshoes.  I had dragged home a young doe only the day before.  I keep large racks of meat seasoning in an upstairs bedroom.  By night many more wild animals moved about, and far more casually than they had at any previous point in my life.

Fair sized packs of coyotes occasionally pass through my view as I hunt the surrounding woods.  Raccoons clear away any left over scraps from the harvested game I leave to the rear of the house nightly.  Already I see that field birds and songbirds seem to be more prodigious.

This last feature I find unusual, as there has not yet been a season to brood, so perhaps it's just that less animals were being killed thus becoming more populous.  There are no longer millions of "domestic" cats killing birds lured to feeders only to be stalked by the family pet. No longer forced to run a gauntlet of claws, rather than freeze to death, the wild birds seem to be thriving.  This seems to make sense and is good enough for me to subscribe to, so I do. Life is comfortable and easy for me here to stay through the winter.

I sit in my chair and reflect on the only love I will ever know. I've written tomes of love letters to Ava. Every word, having been crafted as thoughtfully as if I were carving a bust from solid stone, has been both beautiful and ineffective. I've tried so many ways to articulate my love into writing for her, yet words always fail somehow to find full expression. In the end she'd said it was my words she'd fallen in love with. She said she loved my mind, and through my words she would want her children to remember her by should she be gone; not their own father's. I'd loved her too, which was why the choice she made was one I could have never, and would never have made.

I sit lost in thought on the subject of my love letters. My sight wanders from the bright fire in front of me, to the shelves of books on the far wall. One book, larger than those around it, grabs my attention

It's a large, gray leather bound book, and I can't read its binding from my chair. So I stand up to get a better look. I think of the letters written when I had loved her with my heart on fire, and I wonder what it'd meant of me. But mostly I focus on the very nature of the love letters I had written.

I look down into my hands and recognize the book I'm holding; the *I Ching*. This book predates the Bible by many hundreds of years. It is no doubt a text worthy of a lifetime's endeavor to learn. I have every confidence that greater minds than mine have pondered further into the nature of change and impermanence than I ever could, even if I desired to do so. Which I do not.

It's unavoidable to me, nonetheless, that I have been called to this ancient text. It's intimidatingly thick. I hold it and stroke its pages gently, as a man might stroke a lover's hair as they mindlessly daydream together. I simply ask the book to silence my mind on this subject of those love letters.

I've grown tired of endlessly revisiting in my mind the same dead end avenues. I'm tired of wondering "what if" I'd said or written something differently. I'm hung up on the subject, exactly. I'm not obsessing over it, but I'm ready to let go of it forever and I quite literally think a silent prayer, "Help me. Thank you." I allow my thumb to stop fanning the pages and open the book to whatever one nature chooses.

I open to Book 11: The material. The text I read aloud to myself, and as I do, the hair on my arms stands on end as my question is simply answered. The words I read to myself are these:

*"Writing cannot express words completely. Words cannot express thoughts completely. The Holy sages set up the images in order to express their thoughts completely. They devised the hexagrams in order to express their true and false completely. Then they appended their judgments and so could express their words completely."*

I say out loud to myself, as if filling the role of both master and apprentice, "Love isn't words. It is the works and wonders it creates. Love isn't something you merely speak to someone. Love is action. Love is what it does, not what it says."

I have no interest in bending over the table in the adjoining dining room and painstakingly creating an elaborate mandala to express my words completely upon the large table. I do find great peace flow through me as my recurring thoughts about the words written on the nature of a failed love simply flow out of my mind forever. I slide off the chair into a ball on the floor as I do every night and simply sleep until I'm done.

I walk by a mirror the following day and can't believe my eyes. My first thought is that I look truly happier than I've seen myself in some time. The second thought is that if I owned a diner, I'd put my hand on the pistol under the counter should I walk in and ask myself, "Can I help you?"

I walk through the main street that very day and kick in the door of the barbershop. Let the record show that I do make a point of reaching through, rather than stepping through, the broken door. I open the shattered frame just to hear the bell overhead ring while entering an honest to goodness barbershop.

I walk over to a workstation and without fanfare grab the largest scissors on display. I pull my hair tightly into a ponytail and neatly lop it off. My hair falls to roughly the place where my shoulders meet my neck. It's a horrible cut, and I'm fine with it.

There, next to the door, is an outdoors magazine. I grab it and plop myself heavily into a pivoting barber's chair. I skim through the articles and look at the sunny far away places. For the first time in months I feel the want to stretch my legs beginning to grown in myself. I turn the page and although the magazine opens to a two-paged advertisement I feel my teeth exposed to the cool air as a smile parts my face.

It hadn't even occurred to me, and suddenly it's so obvious. One of the world's most famous outdoor sports shopping destinations is just a casual distance to my west. I confess I'd begun to talk to myself a bit more than would've ever been acceptable before the Righting Moment. I ask myself if I mind. I assure myself I don't. I laugh as I look at the monstrous store pictured in the magazine I hold on my lap, and I say out loud, through a smile, "Adventure awaits."

# CHAPTER 11

A few days later I'm busy making collection runs gathering siphoned gasoline. I acquire a section of hose from a local hardware store for just this task. I find an empty five-gallon bucket that had once contained heating kerosene. This bucket is perfect for transporting my fuel, as it has a screw-on lid on top of a simple pour-spout.

I break into homes as gently as possible, primarily seeking out cars inside of garages. This is for no reason other than it's more comfortable as I wait for the bucket to fill. It's a simple enough task, and I'm done before midday.

Four buckets of fuel have refilled the Land Rover, and I use a portable generator to power a battery charger I found in the municipal works maintenance building. I leave this running and return to the B&B for my children and rifle. I load up the car, buckle up the kids, and turn the key to begin a field trip west to the sporting goods store where I can better outfit my hunter-gatherer's existence.

The car continues to crank until the battery once again needs to be recharged. I'm unsure whether running a fuel injection system as advanced as this one completely dry has resulted in my binding the system. Or, perhaps, gasoline has already begun to break down and form varnish. Either way, I know where a bit less comfortable transportation resides. I gather my simple belongings and walk to a large house on the edge of town.

Parked to the rear of a three bay garage is an old, Vietnam War era Kaiser Jeep M715. Due to their weight rating these old trucks were called five quarters. It looks like an old truck, only bigger.

As I'm placing my belongings into the truck, I notice a propane tank line running into the garage from a small tank. My assumption is validated as I open the side door and see a generator that ties directly into the homes wiring.

The generator winds up to full output without a snag. The battery is more than sufficient to crank up the simple machine. On the wall to the rear of the garage is a breaker panel. I see my way through the switches, following the well-diagramed drawing on the inside of the panel door. Whoever the guy was who owned this house was my kind of people. He would certainly be happy to share some food with a friend.

I head into the home and directly into a large kitchen. I change my mind and return to the breakers and provide power to the inside rooms as well. I boil a large pot of basmati rice, find a can of field peas and some mustard greens, and mix them into the rice. I sit in an electrically lit room for the first time in perhaps ten months. The sound of the generator droning disturbs my senses somehow. I turn off the overhead light because I feel unsettled in its glow. I eat slowly and only as much as I need to feel full.

Back among neatly organized tools I find another battery charger, two extension cords, and a black handled hunting knife in a well-tooled leather sheath. I plug both extension cords into the same outlet and unroll them to the truck. I plug the one cord into the charger and begin to get the batteries back into shape. The other cord I connect to the engine block heater.

I unhook my belt and release two loops worth on my right hip and thread this new knife onto my belt before resetting the buckle. I open the cab and pull out the carbine. I walk into the home and straight down the main hall to the master bedroom. I toss the carbine onto the bed and say to myself out loud, "Fair trade."

Opening the closet on the side of the bed with the men's watch on the nightstand and pulling aside some long winter coats reveals a classic bolt-action rifle stacked into the corner along with a semi-automatic twenty gauge shotgun. On the shelf directly above are two green boxes of shells for the rifle, and three boxes of game loads for the shotgun. I take the whole lot.

I'm willing to bet at this moment, with great confidence, the pistol in the sock drawer is either a service revolver or a colt .45. No need to stop and look though. I have no use for a pistol, and while great fun to fire, they are good for only one thing.

With the presence of all other people removed, both the military carbine and a side arm are now pointless. Certainly there may be a scenario where a pistol is a helpful tool. A large-framed revolver if in the same habitat as bears in the fall, or deep in a swamp with alligators and cotton mouthed moccasins. If the time comes, I'll grab one. Until then, I need only tools for harvesting game.

On the way back to the truck, I make the gesture of taking the rifle from safe to fire several times. This rifle is not my preferred brand, and the safety's not a natural movement. It has a good solid action though; it'll be fine. The shotgun is a different matter. I've never owned a semi-automatic before, having always opted for the simplicity of a twelve-gauge pump. I open up the cab and marvel at how thoughtfully the previous owner has restored this old truck.

Aircraft toggle switches have been installed in place of the original rocker switches. I see that the electrical system is wired in series to power a 24-volt system. That means it has original running gear. That's cool, and worth bragging about at some annual parade. This truck, while pretty much the apex predator of coolness, is deservedly known for unreliability.

I throttle easily through the gears rolling right down through Main Street. The snow is gone, the river is swollen, and redbuds have just started to appear on the trees lining the highway. I've not only lost count of the days going by, I have also lost concern over what day it is. If pressed for a guess, it's the last week of the third month.

From an elevated stretch of highway, passing parallel to the town center of Bethlehem, I allow the truck to roll to a stop. I carry out of the cab with me a Ziploc bag containing the leftovers of my rice concoction. While leaning against the cement side of the highway and looking down into the city, I simply marvel at the beauty I behold.

Directly across the street from the church there is a smoke shop. These shops have always been a gray market. Here you can buy paraphernalia for smoking marijuana. It is simply a game of never saying that your intention is for smoking anything other than tobacco. I've always found it ridiculous how we put in place, and then defend, laws against such a beneficial and kindly plant.

Our culture embraced the mindless slobs we became after having one drink too many. Befittingly, I see a billboard a short distance away where a sleek haired woman of desirable beauty is holding a glass of liquor to her lips. Her eyes clearly say, "One more of these, big boy, and I will lose these pesky inhibitions." And this was true; one more glass of courage, and we'd kill ourselves on the highway, beat each other in the streets, and betray one another in the bedroom.

Yet this simple herb, which I've not smoked in twenty plus years, seemingly has never brought destruction to anyone. Like everything, there are those who'll abuse anything when given a chance. There were always those who possess no natural ability to self-moderate. But to those people, it didn't need to be marijuana. It could be anything: gambling, adultery, shoplifting, or even shameless self-promotion.

I exit the highway at the next ramp, and then backtrack to the street of the church. I look at the green sign hanging over the intersection reading, "Church Street." I roll my eyes as I put my foot to the brake and stop. Idling loudly, parked between the church and the head shop, I let the big diesel enjoy not carrying a load for a moment before shutting it down. I climb out of the cab and walk to the doors where "Aquarian Promise" is painted colorfully on the glass frontage.

As usual, it's a good thing I have on boots as I walk into the shop, since there is broken glass across the floor. To the rear of the store, large glass display cases are locked and full of glass water pipes. "BONGS," I say loudly and laugh.

When this store was occupied, the mere mention of that word would've been forbidden. I would've been made to endure a brief lecture, or asked to leave the store outright. As it is I'm unbothered as I push my boot neatly through the glass case. I grab a rather tall plastic bong, a simple single chamber design, with a sticker of a clown on the tube as subcultural branding.

There's a small office behind a door, which states "employees only," and I open it. Sitting on a chair is a pile of clothes, and I note they are filled with dust rather than ashes. There is literature about medical marijuana dispensaries. I scan the letters. It's apparent this person was risking considerable legal threats trying to facilitate getting medicine to those who were sick and in need.

I notice a vintage-looking messenger bag that is tucked between a small trashcan and the side of the desk. Inside are thin, round aluminum tins with a cam locking mechanism to close them tightly. On the lids of these containers are names, which seem absolutely ridiculous to me. I recognize the effort at snarky humor that this subculture has always attempted to employ; it is one that always fell flatly, in my opinion.

I open one of the tins and inside I find pristine, and odorous, buds of what is obviously high quality marijuana. I slide the tall bong into the bag; on my way out the door I toss several pouches of imported rolling tobacco in as well. I pocket a nice brass lighter, along with a can of lighter fluid that's sitting under the counter.

I walk out onto the street; the sun overhead is shining brightly as I deposit my day's groceries into the truck. I then cross over to the main entrance of this impressive Catholic Church. I find the doors to be solidly locked. A quick search into an alley, yet another felony breaking and entry, and I'm inside of the house of God.

Entering the main cathedral, I'm awestruck at the detail and quality of the stained glass through which the day illuminates this great hall. I head up onto the altar and turn facing the rows of pews. I raise my hands to my sides and say, "Forgive us this day, as we forgive those who trespass against us." I put my arms down and follow up this simple sermon with a heartfelt, "Thank you."

My attention is turned to the large and imposing Bible opened before me on the altar. My curiosity is piqued as I see it is open to the same Psalm I had read once while interring a good friend and mentor into the sea. I clear my throat and imagine that I am speaking to a large hall filled with souls who have gathered just to listen to these words.

## Psalm 107:23-30

They that go down to the sea in ships,
That do business in great waters.
These see the works of the Lord,
And his wonders in the deep.
For he commandeth and raiseth the stormy wind,
Which lifteth up the waves thereof.
They mount up to the heaven,
They go down again to the depths:
Their soul is melted because of trouble.
They reel to and fro, and stagger like a drunken man,
and they are at their wit's end.
Then they cry unto the Lord in their trouble,
and he bringeth them out of their distress.
He maketh the storm a calm,
so that the waves thereof are still.
Then they are glad because they be quiet:
so he bringeth them unto their desired haven.

⚓

It is plainly no coincidence that the last words read from this very Bible are these words; words that I find so familiar. Is this a gently whispered promise that I, too, will be led toward my desired haven? I feel a gentle stirring inside of me and am filled with the urge to both laugh and cry. I walk up the main aisle toward the exit, taking with me a Bible from a rack on the back of a pew as I pass.

The main doors swing open easily when pushed from the inside. I walk somberly down to the truck and reach over to place the Bible into the glove box. Then I'm surprised by how a dashboard can be as large as a kitchen counter without the simple provision of a glove compartment. I slide the Bible into the messenger bag instead, making its contents as unlikely as the buildings that collect to line this very street.

# Chapter 12

A short time later I'm driving over the Schuylkill River. I look up to the castle-sized box store of all that is sporting and consumer. Its faux wood cabin mystic stands proudly in the bright afternoon's sun. A facsimile of nature had been sprayed before the store's front opening with concrete, forming a simulated waterfall that leads into a pond.

I walk past it with my bag over my shoulder, my children inside it now as well, and I see the water is filled with tadpoles. Green things are already forcing their way through every fissure they can find in this façade, and I know it'll soon be wild enough once more.

I fire the shotgun for the first time against the large, clear pane beside the main door. The barrage of tiny lead pellets shatters the glass, which falls to the ground like large hailstones. I step inside and walk through the turnstile. I put my belongings into a green shopping cart and stare in awe at the excess of rampant consumerism.

The first thing most obvious to me is not the airplane, nor the covered wagons, nor the gathering of poly-resin trees, which have been collected to decorate this town-sized shopping center.

It is the gentle, yet pervasive smell of rotten fish. Directly ahead of me, in plain view, is an aquarium of grand stature, its gigantic acrylic walls are stained an impermeable shade of dark green. I need no imagination to visualize what the contents of this display tank must consist of; it is as plain as the nose on my face.

I decide to ditch my weapons in the shopping cart and put my bag over my shoulder. I take a quick inventory of how the different departments are laid out around the store and proceed up a long flight of stairs to several aisles filled with archery equipment. I know bows quite well and will be spending some time here. I place my bag onto the service counter that was laid out for technicians to assist customers. Then I shed all of my foul weather gear.

I select a bow from a hanging rack I would never have splurged on before. I close my eyes and draw it slowly. At full draw, the string comes to rest naturally across my cheek. I walk through the aisles and select all of the other ancillary gear required to build a quality and reliable hunting tool. I go into a safe room intended just for this purpose. I work on the attachments, making many fine adjustments, until it is ready for use in the woods. I place the new bow on the counter and put a dozen arrows, complete with razor bladed broadheads, into a quiver beside it.

I'd intended to go through the weapons and select replacements of the ones I'd stolen in New Jersey. I decide instead to use what I've already acquired. They are simply tools and I feel no need to attach vanity to their name brands, no matter how prestigious they may sound. They are merely implements I need to use to kill food, nothing more.

A bow, however, will range wildly in its speed, its repeatable accuracy, and its reliability. For this reason alone I have spared no effort to use the highest quality components, plus price is no longer an issue. A bow has a much higher likelihood of wounding game, sending an animal off to die painfully for no reason. When I let loose an arrow into a game animal, I want only two things. First, I want a clean and ethical death for a wonderful creature. Second, I want food with which to sustain my body.

I make a thoughtful round of the store collecting any items I may need for whatever road lays ahead of me. Packing for the Appalachian Trail had required a different level of discipline, as I had to carry everything on my back. Then I had a trail to follow and a destination in sight. Now I have no course set before me at all. I do however, have a great big truck. I smile as I open a large marine-grade cooler and casually fill it with foil packages of ready made meals.

I make a rather complete first-aid kit that I outfit within a good quality, roll-topped dry bag. In a section catering to recreational vehicles, I come across a diesel generator and drag it to an area by the entrance where I've begun staging supplies to take with me. I find clothes, tents, a large skillet, boots, and a canoe that I'll strap to the top of the truck.

By the time I've loaded all of my provisions into and onto the truck, darkness is settling in. I go inside to the camping section, fuel, and light off no fewer than eight gas-powered lanterns. Then I place the lanterns in the upper level walkway. I keep one off to the side and leave unlit. Twenty-two years in the military have not been without learning some lessons. I'll have a spare should I need light while refueling the lamps sometime later in the night. What was it those guys in the Coast Guard liked to say? *"Semper Paratus*: Always ready."

I stretch a hammock out of a small stuff sack between the handrails of the wide stairwell. This will have me sleeping suspended over a cement set of stairs, so I'll have to be mindful in the morning.  I unpack a lightweight sleeping bag and lay it out at full length into the hammock.  With my bedroom ready for the night, I go down to the long row of cash registers, which I'm glad I don't need to come square with in the morning for my shopping binge.

Between each row of registers is a small reach-in refrigerator. There are wonderfully colorful sports drinks, thrillingly packaged energy drinks, and large bottles of water.  I grab some water as an idea is crossing my mind.  Smiling to myself, I reach for a second bottle.

I unscrew the lid and draw long pulls of water from the bottle as I walk up the stairs, ducking under my hammock along the way. I walk to the counter on which I've built my bow and retrieve the messenger bag.  I remove the slightly worse-for- wear, yet still in-tact, tubes holding my daughters.  I hold them for a moment trying to convey my love through time, through space, through my sheer will alone somehow to their ears.  "I love you, girls. I am so very proud of you both."

I place them upon the service desk and remove the water pipe. I open the second bottle of water and pour roughly a third into the bong.  Making sure the water level is well below the stem hole.  I cover the carburation hole with my thumb and inhale.

As I'm pulling air through the bong I cover the opening of the pipe's bowl with my left thumb and my breath is stopped solidly.

"Ready for ignition," I laughingly say, as I fish tins of medical marijuana from the bag, opening one, and then two others beside it.  These open tins I put in a row and, sparing myself the drain of reading something Kosmix or Kronik from the labels, I gently handle a bud from each.

One of them captures my senses; its heady aroma is almost sweet, where the other two smell skunkier.  It's as if there's a sheen-like quicksilver hiding in its light green tone. Thin yellow hairs play about the body of the bud with a dusting of fertile resin clinging like dew.

Using the lid of the container it was stored in, I crumble slowly from the end of the large bud. I do this until I've deposited a small pile of herb from which I will smoke. I pull the pipe stem out of the bong and fill its chamber over the tin lid then replace it into the pipe's body. I pull the lighter from my pocket and feel almost too anxious in my excitement. I haven't smoked pot since 1991, and I'm eager to remember what I've been missing.

I hit the bong deeply, slowly, watching bubbles rise through the water then pop into a smoke that hangs heavily inside. I stand up and take a few breaths then fully exhale. Covering the top of the bong with my mouth and sharply inhaling, I clear the chamber of its heavy load of smoke. I try to hold it to be cool out of some old habit; the resulting cough is so powerful, I grab onto my knees and think I may vomit.

There's a familiar tightness in my chest, instantly, as if the whole world's atmosphere has somehow become denser. I do the only thing I can possibly imagine right now. I take two more heavy steamrollers. I put my hands hard to my temples and push my hair back and then rub my eyes with the heels of my palms.

Already I can tell I'd rather not have to roll down the window and produce my license to a frowning highway patrolman. I laugh out loud at this thought. Then I laugh again because only if you were stoned would you find that funny.

Earlier in the day something in the fly-fishing section had caught my eye. I head over that way, hitting my hip on the corner of the counter on the way past. I point at it and declare, "Have that removed!" I snort a laugh at myself then continue on my way back down stairs. I'm back at the workbench in moments holding a machined aluminum fly rod tube. I unscrew the lid then pop the top off of the first cardboard tube.

I hold my breath as I steadily pour the whisper-fine dust from one container into the next. From the backlighting of the gas lamps burning loudly a short distance away, I again see that color, a color I can't describe. It is like greenish purple with yellow flashes.

It is simply the color of magic in my eyes. I imagine it is the spirit of the little girls who once had made fairy houses in the woods behind the house. They are waving their arms saying, "We love you too, Dad."

I screw the lid back onto the aluminum tube and tamp the bottom easily against the counter in a motion similar to the one that might be used to reseat a loose axe hand onto its handle. With the contents settled to the bottom, I pour the second tube into the aluminum one as well. The heart with the diamond falls out, and I stop.

I pull it gingerly from the dusty contents of my precious daughter and empty the remains into the well-engineered container designed for safely transporting thousand dollar fly rods. I mix a small batch of epoxy from the bench holding the tools for assembling compound bows. I then apply a bead of the adhesive around the threads of the cap, tightly sealing the stout aluminum body with authority.

I slide the golden heart off the thin gold chain that once hung on my young daughter's chest. Opening a package containing a black and green bowstring, I thread on the heart pendant and tie it around my neck, binding it with a solid figure-eight knot. I choose this way over a more conventional square knot as a nod to the symbol of infinity. Pulling the string tightly into itself, I seal the bitter ends with the lighter produced from my pocket. Then I sigh heavily.

I close my eyes and breath in deeply three times, letting my breath flow from me through my nose. I hope to pull the weight from my heart out with each released breath; it does not work. I put my hand around the object hanging around my neck; it feels only fitting, as I already wear my heart on the outside.

Ducking under my improvised bed once more, I return to the refrigerator to get another bottle of water. Looking around me, I take in the vast arrangement of mounted fish and wild animals collected throughout this store. In the acid yellow glow of the light cast from loudly hissing lamps, the creatures seem almost as if they're holding still just to fool me, and watching me from every direction at once.

I marvel at how wrong we'd gotten it in the end. Assuming so vainly that we had dominion over all we could destroy. I entertain for a moment sleeping outside in the truck. To be honest, I'm just high enough to find that idea even creepier. I slide my body into the suspended hammock leaving all of my clothes folded on the stairs below me.

Sleep comes as if it has been stalking me. The animals surrounding me are moving as if reanimated in my dreams, and I am unsettled. My thoughts are heavy, and I grow overheated in the sleeping bag I'm zipped inside of—bound as if a swaddled infant. I wake early, drenched in sweat.

Climbing back into the cab of the truck, in the morning I still feel a slight lag in my mind. The marijuana the good doctor had stashed for me to find is truly potent. I shall mix it into rolling tobacco to dilute it, should I desire to partake again in the future.

I don't decide until I pull out back onto the highway if I'll simply return to the library home I've made in Frenchtown. With no conscious decision made, however, I turn right when the moment comes. I head west toward points truly unknown.

I stop my truck next to a tractor-trailer, which had come to rest halfway up a gentle embankment off of the highway. I open the fuel cell under the tractor's cab and siphon diesel from its belly until the fuel overflows from the fill neck on my truck. I drive lazily across mountains that once held small communities, but now have collapsed along with the coalmines they'd been built around.

About the time I wonder if it's my imagination, or if the valve train on the large diesel engine pulling me along is sounding perhaps less inspired, I see signs for an Army National Guard Depot. I follow the signpost to the main entrance, and shepherd this throwback of a military vehicle through tight cement barricades intended to slow exactly an approach such as my own.

Even as I rattle along between cookie cutter buildings painted in a dirty tone of beige, some manual would probably refer to as lemon chiffon, the truck starts to respond sluggishly. Out of the driver's window I can see my shadow rolling predictably beside me, casting a thick line of smoke.

I downshift into a low gear and continue along as the truck begins to surge, bucking occasionally with increasing urgency. I roll the crippled truck into a large parking lot lined with rows of military vehicles. There are armored personnel carriers, large engineering machines, and impressive heavy equipment transports. Most of the vehicles still wear the colors of woodland missions; some are the coyote brown of the desert.

I lumber to a stop in front of a line of tan HHMMWVs, Humvees. I walk over to one and give it a quick once over. A Humvee will be a perfect vehicle for me to carry on with my travels. Its motor is designed well, made to run on various grades of fuel. It'll serve my purposes.

I transfer all of my gear consisting of ammunition, marijuana, and a Bible into the passenger's side seat. I laugh at myself, pondering what possible bumper sticker would best define the driver of this rig: "God, Guns, and Ganga?"

With the canoe strapped solidly onto the back of the truck, I kiss the side of the tube holding my daughters and, as has become ritual, I buckle them into a back seat. Of course, now fully committed to this particular Humvee, the battery won't turn the engine over. No bother. I go through the motions required to get the battery back in service and am soon rolling forward breaking formation with the other vehicles.

Leaving my Humvee idling, and thus further charging the battery, I go over and climb into the old 5/4-ton truck. I coax it back to life and back it proudly into the formation with its brother-in-arms. As I walk back to the Humvee, I see the old truck as if it has been returned onto a pedestal in its proper place in the pantheon.

I stop at the gate exiting the base. I put the truck in neutral and set the brake. I close my eyes and rest my head on arms that are folded over the steering wheel. Since the moment this event has come into being, since the Righting Moment, I've been following only instinct. I need to think of my way to move forward.

Not a life plan, not a list of goals. But a man needs direction, or he is quite simply lost. I cannot just wander and expect to achieve anything. I must find purpose. If I can't find it, then I must at least make purposeful decisions.

I am strongly moved by the image of the old military truck standing proudly alongside of the many vehicles that its genetics were passed along to. I find the thought naturally moves to still more thoughts; thoughts of the genetics that I, too, come from.

My family is an old one.  A grandfather clock in my family's home dates back to 1750.

I think of the mountains that my family had been forcefully displaced from with the creation of the Shenandoah National Park.  It was in 1935 that many families were made to go, to leave lands their families had called home for generations.  It was then that "my people" had been uprooted from the valley carved by the Rapidan River, made to relocate to make room for the park.

I reach down to the gearshift and pull the truck into first, release the brake, and roll out into the world.  I know exactly where I'm going for the first time in many long months.  I'm going to a spiritual home of sorts.

I am going to the Rapidan River.

# CHAPTER 13

It is good, for my travels at least, that the Righting Moment had come in the dark hours. The only traffic on the highway of any consistent nature has been long haul truckers. Without their guidance, most of the eighteen-wheelers had simply come to rest in the median, or had driven off into embanked hillsides.

Several trucks had struck bridge trestles; the damage is never so severe that I can't find a way to pass through with the Humvee. The trucks prove a reliable source of fuel to replace the considerable amount that this truck can burn if I maintain the posted, yet unenforced, speed limit.

I drive straight through the monuments and the grand architecture that had once been the cradle of the experiment known simply as America. Its bold promise, that all men were created equal, had been a beacon of hope during its life. Now suddenly, no words were ever truer. All of mankind is truly equal. Whether reduced to ashes, or dust, I know in my heart was more symbolic than literal. I know everyone has been called home in the end.

I drive south and west from the capital. It's well into the night when I arrive at the retreat President Hoover had built as a getaway from the stress of his position—Rapidan Camp. Ironically it had been his passion, one that I share, and fishing with a fly rod that had helped motivate his decision to displace my ancestors from their homes.

The last section of the drive has been over a gravel stretch of road. Dead fallen limbs and deep rain-carved scars have made their impact felt on the simple road used to access this place. The Humvee is more than up to the challenge, and now sits parked squarely at the bottom of the porch of this presidential getaway.

This place had lost its fancy, in time, to a camp some hundred miles to the north in Maryland. The fact it was a good distance further to travel, and far less accommodating to less adventurous leaders who would follow, proved to save this tiny river. It'd been designated officially as a wilderness area many years later. And its waters were closed to the harvesting of any fish for the first several miles of its flow over free rocks and huge boulders alike.

I pry the locks off the door with a Halligan bar I'd grabbed from one of the other vehicles I'd inspected before choosing the truck that I left in. I walk into the darkened main building of the camp. The sound of the river flowing by gently fills the air inside with murmured promises; a Barred Owl nearby asks, "Who cooks for who, who cooks for you?"

I opt to sleep outside in a tent. I'll take the time in the morning to make this building into a camp ready for its new, less presidential, inhabitant later. I walk down to the river through blackness and kneel awkwardly on a large boulder. I fill my hands with icy cold water and splash it across my face and neck.

I then cup my hands around my mouth as I had in Vermont, and again I call out to a bird. Only this time, I ask the same question it had asked. Who does cook for who? I smile into the night, unseen, as it answers with predictable redundancy.

It seems this simple question is the only concern in the whole world tonight. Tomorrow I shall go into the woods with my bow. Then, if I'm lucky, I will answer the question of who cooks for whom. I shall do so upon the porch that I've just walked across. I climb into my sleeping bag, zip the tent closed, and fall asleep in a small clearing in the woods my ancestors had once called home.

There are fiddleheads coming up on the sides of the valley formed by the river. I kill a young yearling buck with a well-placed arrow, which passes straight through his chest. The arrow has gone on to bury itself so deeply into a small beech tree that I have to unscrew the broadhead, recovering only the arrow's shaft. I fry the fiddleheads in fat rendered from the young deer's lean meat.

The trees have begun to bud leaves in earnest now, and insects begin to show again on the wind. A large black bear sows through the woods, behind her follow two newly minted cubs. I sit in silence and watch as they tumble in playful battle as their mother tears greedily into the ground for soft tubers.

It's good here; I feel centered, and the air itself seems to carry old and familiar smells. I have neglected one thing, though, during my shopping spree at the box store of all that is outdoors. I'd had actually walked right into, and then right out of, the fly fishing section and had not thought to procure a rod.

I capture small beetles and millipedes from under rocks and drop them into the river. I sit and watch them drift through small seams in the current where they are plucked away without warning by the trout, always eagerly watching for opportunities to come floating by.

One afternoon I walk further over the ridges then I previously have ventured. I come across an old cabin of sorts that is settling back into the woods it was built from. It's still standing, though barely, and the sun comes in freely through its failed roof. There are nails on the wall from which I can imagine people had once hung their items. I don't get the feel that it'd ever been a home.

Judging by the site on which it was built, the view from its single doorway, and the thoughtful joinery of the logs at its corners, it had been crafted with great care. I pull a small notepad from my pants pocket, along with the military ballpoint I'd found in the Humvee. I put the pen to the paper, take one last look through the door at the view of the river valley, and I write this short poem.

Fingers turn leaves on a windy hillside,
closing on loam; just a stone left inside.
Hands into pockets of pants walking away,
a piece of home proffered for some other day.

Soon rains will fall on this dirty tin roof,
where Grandma's cough syrup was a cool ninety proof.
Ginseng dried hollow on a bent penny nail,
"sing" the men called it; "put's wings on a snail."

Thin clouds drive by quickly,
high in a sky of bunting blue.
It's going to rain hard,
in the next day... maybe two.

But right here, right now is perfect,
before the storm starts to show.
To stand simply watching,
The slow parade of the Rapidan's flow.

# CHAPTER 14

Sitting on the porch, my bare feet propped on the handrail, I lean back easily into the chair I brought out from the main building. I watch as a small trout comes from behind a large stone in the gentle stream and rises to take emerging insects from the surface as they pass.

The simplicity of its existence is so powerfully pure. It knows no calendar aside from the types and frequency of the forage it feeds upon. Its body feels no pressures to perform other than the seasonal rises and falls of the water in which it lives.

The very temperature of its environment drives its metabolism. When it is cold, there is less to find to sustain itself, so it slows down. Its body will come into full power as the bounty provided for it comes to into full bloom, in the form of large hatches of insects in the heat of the summer sun.

One could sit here forever and watch the full cycles of this humble creature's life. However, I feel the urge to keep moving just as the headwaters of the river before me. I collect my few belongings back into the truck. Then I bring out the remains of the young buck that's been kept hanging in the rear of the main building. The carcass is deposited on the ground at the bottom of the stairs.

It has always been a shame to waste food. In the world I now live in, there is no such shame. There will be no waste here. Though I took the young deer's life, it is being gifted through me right back to all of creation.

Within minutes there will be flies that will seek to lay their eggs upon the meat. Shortly after there will be a buzzard who spies the carcass from the thermals it is riding far above. It will draw more buzzards; the attention will attract coyotes, or a bear.

What is left in the end shall be pushed into the soil during the next series of rains. There it will be further digested into the roots powering the plants to grow. The plants will feed the next young buck to fill the void left by the last one. No, here there is no waste, and there is no shame in that.

I roll out of the valley and off of the gravel road back through the small pocket farms that'd gained such favor in these hills between the cities. Soon enough I'm entering the college town of Charlottesville. The markings of the outskirts of the city are the telltale chain restaurants; the same box stores that'd made their mark on every community by the end.

To the rear of one large shopping center, I see a simple sign for an independently owned fly fishing outfitter. I pull the Humvee to a stop half on the road, half on the sidewalk, and push in the front door with my bumper. I back away, coasting to a stop against a light post.

I walk in through the door hanging helplessly by the top hinge. I take in the sights of a very well appointed store; I see the place had obviously been a source of great pride to its owners. It's tastefully decorated in hardwood and green. The front counter is well appointed with art and glossy photographs. The pictures show people grinning as they pursue a passion, deeply held.

Displayed in the front of the store are the highbrow brands of clothes I always associate with those who feel compelled to dress for their lifestyle. Not unlike how the culture surrounding motorcycles had developed a uniform, ironically, to designate its fervor for individuality. So too had the angler adopted a uniform. Only the angler's earth-toned palette of colors was somewhat more diverse than black leather and denim, but not by much.

An incredible selection of finely made fishing hardware is located to the rear of the store. I select a quick action four-piece rod that breaks down into a flannel lined aluminum tube. From a large display case I select a reel.

Into the pack, I also put boxes of line. I grab enough specialty tools that I'll undoubtedly wind up culling some of them out later. I also snag a book that caught my eye on the rivers of the surrounding area.

I find a large aluminum fly box that I painstakingly line with a thoughtful arrangement of flies to simulate the full spectrum of the lifecycle of flying insects, and a few crawling ones as well. A second large fly box I supply with large bass poppers, baitfish simulating streamers, and large meaty flies with conical brass heads. Satisfied with a full selection of flies I locate a pack, which is worn on the chest to make all of this accessible while fishing.

There is a workbench on the back wall of the shop, and I notice a nautilus shell that has been cleanly cut into a cross section. I bring the polished shell into my hand and turn it over in my palm. Of all of the whispers the God of creation has placed before in our ears, few are less subtle than a simple ratio named for its discoverer. In the book *Liber Abaci*, its author, Fibonacci, introduced the world to the Golden Ratio. Some would go on to say that it was the very language of God. The Golden Ratio is simply a progression of numbers, each added to the one before to create the next number: 1, 1, 2, 3, 5, 8, 13, etc.

The simple arched curve that this formula creates can be seen throughout nature with uncanny frequency. It forms the spiral of hurricane, the alignment of nuts in a pinecone, the very shell I hold in my hand. The mathematics of this deceptively simple formula have held influence over the stock market, are found in the proportions of almost all life on Earth, and in the way I tie a leader for fly fishing.

Years ago I'd experimented with both day trading on the internet, and tying my own leaders for fly fishing. I had researched considerably and never found another person who used the Golden Ratio in building a leader. My logic was that if it were, in fact, the perfect ratio, it would be optimal to help ease my attempts at developing a better cast. My secret hope was that if it was indeed the language of God, it might help bring me more bites.

After selecting lines from large spools hanging readily on the wall, I build three leaders each nine feet in length. The first numbers in the Golden ratio are 1, 1, 2. By taking nine feet and breaking it into three sections I have the formula that 2.25 feet added to 2.25 feet equals 4.5 feet. Those three sections tied together give me the desired nine feet overall in keeping with the ratio Fibonacci had discovered in the year 1202.

A fly fishing leader is built from increasingly thinner sections of line in order to best carry the energy from the line to the fly at the end of the cast. There is a careful balance required to be able to "turn over" larger flies yet present them with minimal disturbance to wary fish. To select the weight of each section, I go on to use the next numbers in the Golden ration: 1, 2, 3.

The leaders I'm tying are for Smallmouth Bass in a river, so I opt for an eight pound breaking strength at the thinnest section. This represents 1. Section two will be simply twice section one, so I pull a sixteen pound line down to use next. This is section 2. The final, and longest section is the butt section of the leader that will tie directly to the fly line. Section three will again be double the weight rating of the previous section. Since a sixteen-pound line was used in section two, and I have never seen a thirty-two pound test line, I pull a spool of thirty pound line down. This is section 3.

I don't know if Fibonacci or his Golden Ratio are truly a whisper of God's language. I can say with all certainty that my casting improved rapidly with the leaders of my own dimensions. As to whether God himself has any interest in the frequency of my hooking fish, I have my suspicions that he does not.

On a display case near the cash register I find a small leather wallet designed to hold fly fishing leaders, and I place my three neatly coiled leaders inside of it. I gather up the remaining items that caught my interest and load them into the rear seat of the truck. Walking over to the store's broken door, I lift it by its handle and replace it into the frame; the first such deference I've shown, and I do it out of respect to the previous owner.

# Chapter 15

**B**efore leaving Charlottesville, I follow the signs and drive right up onto the front yard of Thomas Jefferson's house. The lawn is overgrown; the trees are already unkempt. The encroachment of wilderness upon this home's walls only adds to the striking mark it has on this hillside overlooking the Rivanna River.

Climbing onto the large hood of the Humvee, I begin reading different sections of the book written specifically to give guidance on fishing the Rapidan River.

My attention cannot avoid being pulled to the domed structure before me. Thomas was a man who'd once scoured the text of the Bible and created his own edition. He said that finding the truth of the Bible was as easy as finding diamonds in a dung heap. He'd been a Deist, believing in a God of nature. Even being so forward in his thinking toward this end that he would pen into the Declaration of Independence, "The Laws of Nature, and of Nature's God." This would be the only mention of God in the entire text.

Thomas Jefferson had conceived the journey of Lewis and Clark. This man would go on to create the Virginia Statute for Religious Freedoms. He was so prodigious of an inventor that in

1790 he created the Patent Act, something I always found as ironic as it was genius.

My grandfather, who considered Thomas Jefferson the greatest American in history, made this man thoroughly known to me. My grandfather, too, was a man steeped in both science and nature. He would always note with an approving nod toward Thomas Jefferson that, "The man had so loved his country that he died on the Fourth of July."

My look once more affixed to the book in my hands, I begin to lay out a simple plan to fish what seems to be a promising section of the Rapidan River. The only foreseeable problem is that it will require the need to make a very long walk back to my vehicle, or the need to figure out some method of having a shuttle vehicle to utilize. Why this is a dilemma in my mind is unclear to me; it isn't like I have somewhere else to be.

Nonetheless, I hatch a plan and it all makes sense. I drive first to an automotive parts store. I grab a bucket, a large funnel, some hoses, and a large fuel filter. Using this simple device, I'm able to siphon and clean gasoline in one pass. Filtering around three gallons proves to be my limit before the boredom kills my interest in collecting four. With a bucket of good fuel sloshing on the floor beside me, I drive cautiously to a Honda dealership across the street.

In the service area to the rear of the dealership I find several bikes still in their crates from the factory. One of them is a small 125cc dirt bike, and I quickly mix two-stroke oil into the gasoline and fill its tank. After a quick inspection, and filling the tires with air, I'm able to get it running. I toss it into the bed of the Humvee and head off toward Elly's Ford and a day on the Rapidan.

Almost to the river, I find the open pastures of the battlefields of Chancellorsville impossible to stay off of with the Humvee. The grass there has grown tall already, and as I roll across these once-bloodied fields, there is a peace that is palpable. In the distance is a line of civil war era artillery set in a hillside, and I throttle off to investigate them.

I imagine what it would've been like to be defending that redoubt ahead of me, and seeing a coyote brown Humvee barreling across the grass; the thought makes me smile. Coming over a small rise finds me frantically standing on the brakes with both feet, the Humvee leaving four fresh skids of torn earth beneath it. The truck grinds to a stop with its front grill only inches from the sharpened logs that line the base of the civil war redoubt. Large, roughly pointed logs have been rebuilt to simulate the time period of war.

I climb out to investigate, imagining an impact that would've destroyed the freedom of my mobility. I think of the horses and men who would've once stacked up to fight and die against logs just like these; it is grotesque and unthinkable to me. But it happened, and right here, that almost two hundred thousand Americans met bent on bringing one another to their ends. These same fields are still scarred from the wheels of artillery and saw no less brutal carnage in the fighting of the Revolutionary War less than a century earlier.

It's always been difficult for me to understand why the celebration of these two dark red stains on this continent's history are not more richly celebrated for what they truly were. They were both essentially the same battle, they were both won, and they were both vitally important in the process of social evolution. Both of these two wars were a simple declaration, braving the power of their era, to be heard at the risk of seemingly certain peril; the declaration that all men are made equal and free.

America would always wear the period of slavery, which preceded the Civil War, as a black band of shame upon her sleeve. Yet slavery was an institution older than the story of Moses, older than the pyramids his enslaved people had built. Slavery was an evil incarnate upon this earth since the dawn of history. Within less than a century, its hold on mankind would forever be broken. Slavery would be abolished when pitted against the will of a people who stood for the simple words that Thomas Jefferson had penned. The words of a nation's independence, that all men "Are endowed by their Creator with certain unalienable Rights, that among these are Life, Liberty, and the pursuit of Happiness."

Should it have really been so difficult in the end for people to see this? That while as vile and evil as slavery has always been, it was not a black eye on the face of this nation. The abolition of one of mankind's most pure sins from upon this very soil was in fact among America's finest achievements as a country.

This is a thought so contrary to the popular notion held in the time I'd lived in, before the Righting Moment, even *thinking* it would've cast me as out of touch with reality. The culture I had lived in was one that felt bound instead by a mark of shame. When held in honest evaluation, the pride of this accomplishment should've been carried on proud banners at every corner. We were a country who fought so ferociously to be free. Then we chose to live without the very freedoms gained after such incredible sacrifice.

Pulling the Humvee into the parking lot of Elly's Ford only minutes later, it has already grown too late to begin my exploration of this section of the river. I sit quietly in the cab of my truck and work at rigging the rod I will carry in the morning. I roll a considerable joint from one of the other tins I have with me, just for good measure.

A rabbit is chewing fresh clover at the far end of the parking lot, having hopped into the clearing several minutes after I shut down the Humvee. I walk casually and without stopping, a trigger to a rabbit's defense. There is a single report from the shotgun. Before long, the rabbit is releasing pleasant aromas across the woods, suspended over a simple campfire splayed out upon peeled green oak limbs.

# Chapter 16

The morning comes gently as I stir awake in the cab of the truck. I drive down to the point I intend to exit the river with the completion of my days fishing, and drop off the dirt bike to wait for me here. Returning to Elly's Ford without fanfare, quickly I outfit myself for the day wearing only shorts, an old Grateful Dead T-shirt, and the chest pack filled with my angling necessities.

As I step into the river, I feel my perceptions change as I am evolved into a higher level of awareness of the life around me. I feel the flow of the water that had been gin clear, and cold as the grave, in the mountains to my west. Here the water is a thin turbid green, still quite clear, but carrying particulates from the farm-lands built too tightly against its banks.

I sit on a small sandy island that temporarily parts the river into two smaller streams. Slowly, in lightly drawn tokes, I smoke down the thick smoke of the joint I've rolled. Even these tokes I make effort to thin, drawing air through my nose. This is an effort to keep the high that I reach tempered from gaining the cerebral stoning I know this potent herb is capable of creating. By the time I stand up, flicking the burnt stub of the cigarette into the river, I am deeply and comfortably high.

Huge sections of the river have been scarred by erosive destruction for what will be many years to come. Sand from the
fields have filled the crevices of granite bedrock that once made
the bottom of this river a bastion for a diverse aquatic life. Now
these sections are barren. So I wade easily along with the river's
gentle encouragement. I walk until the water enters sections of
lake-like stillness, and into these I merely continue until my buoyancy carries me long.

I lie back and watch the limbs of huge sycamores pass by
overhead. A kingfisher drops from a limb and takes into the hunt
headfirst, rising into instant flight with a small sunfish pierced in
its bill. High above, turkey Buzzards ride as lazily as I float below
them; their sharp eyes scan for a meal through the canopy of trees.

I feel completely at home here. I belong in this time and in
this moment. I see schools of ocean running shad in the deeper
sections as they dart by beneath me. A Great Blue Heron watches
me with cautious eyes as I float by as if in a dream.

I was eleven when I had my first independent, and genuinely
spiritual, thought. I thought then that the God of Creation would
never ask me to supplicate myself indoors on such a day as this,
just to pay it homage to it. Creation is an action, it is purposeful,
and it demands nothing, it deserves only gratitude. So I say the
words, "Thank you," as I float on through this sermon in the place
I have always called my Church.

Embraced by the water, held aloft as if in a safe cradle, I hear
nothing of the world around me but the movement of the very
water I am suspended in. I think of this world I am so genuinely lucky to be part of. I think of where it had been the night I
was awakened by the fall of an airliner. I marvel at how far off
from the point we had journeyed, how far away from the lives we
should've been living together all along.

We had built a life so full of static that we could no longer hear the whispers in the wind, nor discern the babble in a brook. These inklings were always busily nudging us in the form of coincidence, brief moments of familiarity, perhaps hidden in a smell, or a warm breeze across our skin.

We saw only our own selves, even as we were surrounded by so many. So busy with our day planners, the appointment with a teacher, the credit card's score, and a passport photograph, that we never saw the 'check engine' light was burning brightly on the dashboard all the while. Always distracting us was the blaring ambient droning of constant traffic as we sped forward always desperately seeking only be somewhere else.

We'd manufactured a world where energies were transmitted carrying boorish personalities making prank calls, and inescapable portable phones which blinked mindless messages without pause. The very vehicles on which these energies travelled not only went through cement walls to their receivers, but right through the very skulls containing our dreams.

We'd filled our own visions with flashing lights selling a perfection we could never attain. Young girls would push their fingers down their throats to look like the girls in those very images who pushed their fingers down their throats as well. A false Deity had been sucking the marrow from our collective suffering; his name was "Greatness."

We saw ourselves as the master, staking our claim solidly through the destruction of that which had already made us as perfection. We would put poison into our homes, our water, and our very own blood in an effort to destroy everything that we saw as beneath our own self-idolizing image. With it all long gone, I imagine I can feel diatoms spinning through the water I flow within. I am becoming them, as they replicated themselves, using the very elements from the sweat being washed from my pores.

I, too, will lie still one day as my bones are picked over and flown off to a nesting brood. With absolute certainty, I shall sink back into the mass of creation on a world that will be absorbed as well in its own time, back into the clouds of infinity. A child can imagine when an elephant hears a Who. But what happens when a Who hears a Who, and that Who hears one too?

I am jolted from this sunshine daydream as something large and firm hits my feet. In the moment I take to gather my senses I splash about like an idiot, as I finally stand upright on the wide rock ledge I have floated down upon. Collecting my wits for a moment, I take in the scenery around me.

The river takes a long turn to the south before me. The structure of the banks, and the bottom alike, are different here. Here the river has cut deeply into a raised ridgeline into solid granite bedrock. The river has thick beds of aquatic plants holding solidly to a hard rock floor. This is the river I came to seek, of which I'd read promises so eloquently written in the book I'd stolen in Charlottesville.

I wade down into a shallow flow with a sharp drop-off below it. I see baitfish holding tightly to the structure along its edges for protection. Deep cuts through the rock provide passages between deep holes smoothly carved into the stone by centuries of slow erosion. I watch, and I feel, as the currents carry water into places so overwhelmingly beautiful I am temporarily unable to do anything but grin like a fool.

First loosening the drag on the reel, I pull the line through each of the eyes down the length of the rod. Onto the end of the leader I tie a large green and yellow streamer that has thick rubber "legs" and a bright copper conical head to help deliver it into the depths

I will fish.

# CHAPTER 17

An ancient sycamore tree leans comfortably over the river's far bank. The patchwork texture of its bark breaks the outline of the giant tree's trunk. A massive network of roots grows out of the riverbank. Having grown outside of the support of the earth, into water, they then double back onto themselves as they reach into the soil.

The root wall under a sycamore is a universe unto itself. Thousands of deep tunnels into a living wooden bank provide concealment to creatures ranging from rare spiders, to the occasional River Otter. Crayfish seek shelter backed into smaller crevices, into which by night raccoons will stick their arms looking to find them. I know too, that these target rich locations are a preferred haunt of my quarry: the Smallmouth Bass.

In an effort to keep my intentions secret to the denizens I hope are on patrol around the tree's base, I climb out of the river on the opposite bank. The need to be vigilant is constant in the woodlands of Virginia. Pulling my torso over the rivers bank and holding the base of a young tree as if choking it, I look around me to ensure the next handhold doesn't rattle before biting.

There is no rattlesnake, no copperhead, and no water moccasin; there is dense poison ivy. If given the choice between poison ivy and a petulant urinary tract infection, I would call it a draw. If choosing between exposure to poison ivy, and exposure to the quarry I'm stalking, I have not a moment of hesitation. I make a conscious effort to keep my head above the glossy green leaves, using a stick from the ground to part the plants as I pass.

I come over a gentle rise at the bottom of which a small stream enters the river. In the shallow hollow created by this tiny brook there is a large stand of jewelweed, gathered in what I have always called a hammock.

Before the Righting Moment, most people couldn't have told you poison ivy from jewelweed; there was no need, as we had paved ourselves into isolation. If one were to venture too far out and be exposed to poison ivy, say on a small mulched section between shopping centers, there were aerosol cans filled with effective chemicals to abate the irritating itch. Here, there is jewelweed, and I hope my awareness will have avoided me a single scratch.

First I wash my hands and forearms using mud from the stream's bank, removing as much of the ivy's oil from my skin as possible. Once I have completely rinsed the mud away, I gather a large bundle of fresh jewelweed.

I then knead the plant between my hands in a crushing motion similar to one I'd use to soften clay before molding it. The juice of the plant runs between my fingers as I wipe it thoroughly into my face, my neck, and down my arms. It's probably unnecessary, as I am fairly resilient to poison ivy, but it's prudent, so I do it.

Reentering the river with a smooth drop into water just over my head, I pull myself, using a slow sidestroke to an outcropping of rocks. Gravel and sand form a tongue-like peninsula just under the water. I wade along this stony sandbar, against the flow, until

I am immersed only up to my crotch. Less than seventy feet away the roots of the sycamore form the river's bank, only separated by a deep green hole.

I strip several long pulls of line from the reel and flip the rod in my wrist as if I was skipping a stone. Smoothly, and in long powerful movements the line is paid out and streaming through the air. I focus on a place just upstream where the river's flow stalls against the deeper pool. Pulling the line forward first with the rod, then with a double hauled motion from my other hand, I cast almost the full length out onto the water river.

The leader I have tied does its job as the energy is carried forward like a small wave breaking easily along a sandy shore. The weighted fly breaks the surface almost ninety feet in front of me. Hand tending the slack from the line, I flip a large arch forward and upstream. This will allow the lure to sink freely; the tended line comes to be straightened by the river's flow even as my lure reaches the depths I seek to probe.

The weighted fly drops out of sight, and I estimate its position by the amount of line that has sunk into the deeper water below. Careful management must be employed to control the slack. Artificially influencing the drift of the fly with too much tension alerts game fish to something unnatural; allow too much slack and the lure will be hit, tasted, and spat out without anyone being none the wiser.

When I had originally transitioned from more modern tackle to fly fishing, I had missed many good opportunities due to the habit of trying to set the hook too quickly. I'd been trout fishing in a small stream in California when a fellow who happened to be nearby walked up to me. He apologized, acknowledging instantly it was none of his business. I knew he'd watched me miss two fine fish in a row; I smiled and nodded for him to proceed.

He said, "I can tell you are a gear fisherman, because you set the hook like it is a competition. When you see the fish rise to your fly, first thank God, then raise the rod." The next time one of these high mountain trout flashed, I said, "Thank you," and raised the rod. Man and fish alike noticed the difference instantly. Truly "Praise God, raise the rod" is more eloquent; to me, it's just a bit too redundant though. I've never done a thing in my life with a fishing rod other than praise God.

I make two more casts into this same section of the river. With each cast I proceed a little further into the pool, trying to minimize disturbing the whole area too quickly. I shift my focus over to the wall of roots itself and place the fly only inches from the mass of tangled wood. No sooner is the line tended back under control when it twitches as if shocked along its entire length.

Out of memories deeply embedded, I pause only a moment then raise my right hand, with the rod in my grip, as if in class trying to get a teacher's attention. For a moment the weight on the rod has me thinking I may've become snagged on the roots. Then the line begins moving slowly up the current, and I feel the pulse of the pressure as the fish bends its body to swim.

The fish is heading straight into the center of the tangled roots, and I swing the rod over as if directing traffic the other way, pointing its tip away from the fish, and stalling its forward movement. In a flash of bronze and turbid green spray, the fish breaks out of the depth into the air; it is Mr. Redeye himself. Mister Redeye is the name I give any Smallmouth Bass that I think may best the magic mark of twenty inches.

The Bass is deceptively powerful for its size. With every forward run it moves water with the power of a deeply braced canoe paddle. It employs cunning tricks of wild direction changes, has bursts of speed on par with any saltwater predator, and has one trait I've never found another fish to possess: a Smallmouth Bass simply does not run out of fight.

In short order, despite its best efforts, I coax it to swim past me too closely and dart my hand into its mouth, lifting it from the water by its lower jaw. I am careful to allow the fish to hang freely minimizing the risk of damaging the structure of its jaw. It is glorious to behold and brightly alive.

I look upon the sheer majesty, the beauty of the craftsmanship brought into action creating such an amazing thing. I stare at the bounty of this place, which created the circumstances for this animal to evolve so wonderfully designed to hunt from the apex in its river home. The fish's glossy blood-red eye merely looks at me blankly. Dark barring marks its face breaking its outline. Vertical bars of deep bronze and golden brown brand its flanks.

I return him slowly into the water, holding its head into the current, and let go. It remains in place, its mouth still lightly closed on my thumb, and now he holds me until the decision to release is made of its own volition, not mine. The bass flexes its jaw, perhaps to work out the cramp of being held aloft by it, and slowly moves away from me.

With a broad stroke of its tail, it splashes water at me and then disappears. I know perfectly well that it did neither hold me, nor splash me, in a conscious manner. Mr. Redeye does this to me, however, more often than not; the persistence has me growing suspicious.

# CHAPTER 18

Three sharp kicks on the little dirt bike's starter, and I'm racing off in a cloud of dust. The angry report of the small two-stroke engine sounds as alien as would any flying saucer through these mellow woods. I feel a vacuum of sorts created around me as I disturb everything within earshot. Winding dangerously quickly down a gravel road back toward the Humvee, tears running down my cheeks from my watering eyes, I feel playful and more lighthearted than I have in a long time.

Ahead of me, up a cleared hill from the road, is a small and simple home. It occurs to me that of all the things we'd invented by the end, none was more purposefully designed than the humble toilet. I ride the small dirt bike up three cement stairs onto the porch at the front of the house. Sitting next to my feet there is a hand painted garden gnome, his bright red pants already fading to pink unprotected from the sunlight.

I'll have to be careful walking in after the gnome's trip through the glass-paneled front door, as I am barefoot. Had I thought it through, I would've left boots with the dirt bike. Riding a motor-cycle barefoot is an incredibly good way to lose your math skills five percent at a time.

After using the toilet, and being stunned to find the tank holding enough water after all this time to flush, I set off to find a pair of shoes. The small bedroom contains the remains of the couple who lived here. It is a humble home and I see, with a casual glance, that the shadows on pillows are of dust.

The pair of work boots are two sizes too big, and they flap on my feet as I walk into the kitchen to find some canned food. There are a few cans of vegetables, and a large, handled bottle of whisky. I eat the canned vegetables and then set off cradling the bottle of booze awkwardly between my knees.

I ride into the parking lot with the Humvee just as it is getting dark enough so that I'm forced to slow my pace. Leaning the bike against a nearby tree, I set about reorganizing my tackle into proper places in my vehicle. Pulling the tube filled with my daughters out of the back seat, I carry them to a large rock by the river and sit down.

There is no moon out tonight and thin clouds obscure the stars, darkening the sky still further. I put down the aluminum tube and tell my daughters, "Let me go light a fire, then I'll tell you about my day." Other travelers here have collected an ample pile of wood in days now gone. I put fire to a large stacked pyramid of logs with the brass lighter. The gasoline I tilted out of the bike's tank and into the woodpile barks as the fire grows to life quickly.

I take a deep swallow from the bottle of whisky; its warmth glows into my chest, and the woody vapor rises into my nose. Returning to my seat by the river, I place my daughters on my lap, and take another long pull from the bottle.

"If I could sing, I would sing you a song about Bass. Just like my Great Grandfather did for me, when I was young." I smile down toward them, imagining they are smiling back. Then I think for a moment of a song and add, "But you know I won't lie; I can't sing worth a damn."

I tell the girls about the poison ivy as if the knowledge might still be useful to them one day. I tell them of how my cast had not abandoned me despite its long period of neglect. Tears fill my eyes. I miss them badly, and I am deeply and heavily lonely. Without even noticing, I have drained several inches of whisky from the bottle. I rise to observe the time honored rite of pissing into the fire, and I stumble, tripped up by my own two feet.

Returning from the call of nature, I settle deeply into the large stones by the river. I am remarkably drunk, my head is doing loops, and I hold my children tightly to keep them from spinning off my lap. I close my wet eyes and breathe slowly; the rocks I'm sitting among seem an appropriate bed for my heavy heart.

Sleep has no intention of providing any respite from my lonely thoughts, and soon I am dreaming of days from my youth. The dreams are clear, unaffected by the influence of the spirits coursing through my veins. I'm in an old car, a convertible; the sun of early summer warms the rich black interior. Next to me a good friend smiles at something I've said; it helps me settle even further into the riverbank that she is beautiful.

We are both playfully high, and laugh without reservation. There is an easy, comfortable feeling between us as we walk over an earthen dam away from view from the parking lot. We plop down beside each other into the thick grass as we speak of things only young men and women could recall.

The hillside is covered in a backdrop of buttercups, their bright yellow contrasting magically against the rich green ground. She smiles at me and laughs; the most infectious laugh I've known. Her bright, almond shaped eyes are the color of raw wildflower honey. I am inspired by her eyes, and also feel as scared as if held at gunpoint. The tension between us has been growing for a long time, and then our hands meet each other's as we lie closely together.

This simple touch proves to frustrate the conversation into an awkward pause; it's our cue, and we get it. Together, without a word, we move to each other and kiss. Our kiss is shallow at first, awaiting the other to protest. Then the pace quickens, the caresses grow in intensity, until the time comes when a transition into further engagement seems appropriate. But, I falter at this moment.

I would never have admitted it then, as sexual conquest is the most highly embellished of all teenaged endeavors. I'd been sexual with only one girl, and only one time at that. I knew of no way to make my move upon her as I so desperately desired. Instead, I made awkward conversation of how it wasn't the right place, or time, or some other nonsense, believing all the while it was the right time exactly.

I wake to the knowledge that I am fully aroused. I'm also woefully hung-over, have to urinate rather ferociously, and my mouth tastes like I've eaten raw wild mushrooms. The girls sit safely lodged between two large stones where they, undoubtedly, made off to in the night to escape the fumes of my exhaust.

I step out of my clothes and walk directly into the river. The flow is shallow here, and I lie on my back in the gravel and let the water wash across me for a long time. I'm hurting in a new way, and it is growing in me. The developing heaviness on my heart is similar to the way this river swells after a hard rain forces the restraints of its banks. Rather than being washed from me, as I'd hoped, loneliness seems to seep into me from the water itself.

Unceremoniously, I put dirty clothes back on; a mental note is made to find some clean ones. I place the girls into the restraint of the back seat. Then I walk over to ensure the fire is fully doused.

Then I pick up the bottle of whisky, spin violently, and then throw it full force into the grill of the Humvee. I'm not sure why. Glass and liquor fly off in every direction. The only consolation of this destructive act is the thick fumes of whisky. The pungent mist suspended in the air burns my eyes, at least temporarily justifying my flowing tears.

This random act of destruction has done nothing to stave off my growing rage. Stomping in oversized boots, I get onto the bike and kick the starter. With my head filled with unsettling angst, that and a solid hurting from the booze, I toe through the gears quickly flying across the bridge that spans the river immediately out of the parking lot. Perhaps a rowdy blitz on this bike down some forgotten back road may release some of the tension.

Standing up on the pegs I watch the river pass quickly under me as I throttle hard around a tight curve in the road. To my left, through a line of trees, I see a gravel road that cuts through a thick stand of cedars along the river's far edge.

The clutch is pulled in. I step down two gears and popping the clutch breaks the rear tire loose, and the bike begins to slide. I lean into the turn and rolling hard onto the throttle launches me in a new direction, toward the entrance to the gravel road. The small bike is deceptively quick, and I am riding without the restraint of self-preservation.

A steel chain has been hung between the trees to stop poachers, or to keep summertime kids from swimming naked in the river beyond. The chain, now thickly covered in brown rust, has hidden effectively until the moment to reveal itself was at hand.

The chain meets the bike at the stem of the frame and instantly, savagely, I am thrust forward and into the air.

I land on my knees, but momentum only throws me back into the air now spinning wildly. The sudden stop is mind numbing, as I'm driven into the base of a large tree. My back hits first; wind is knocked from my lungs like a piñata being hit by a train. My head slams into the tree with amazing force. My mouth is filled with the taste of pennies; my vision flicks to gray and then snaps back into focus.

My eyes recognize what they see as the front wheel of the bike, only in time to close themselves tightly as if to hide. The wheel has broken free from the forks upon impact; it takes one last skip off the gravel road before hammering straight into my face. The wheel drives my head again into the tree with all of the pent-up eagerness of a chubby kid swinging at a ball on a tee. There is no hesitation. There is no hurt.

There is nothing.

# CHAPTER 19

Behind her burqa a nineteen-year-old girl cries. The outside world viewed as if through the division of a confessional. Her eyes are granted further mercy by the tears that rush to fill them. Made vague are the details of the torn and ruined body that was once her infant daughter.

Her hands fumble, trying wildly to reassemble. Wracked by unbridled convulsions, her ribs punch deep bruises into her tender young thighs. Through the corner of her vision, a dusty suede boot passes. In a voice too alien for her to understand, a young man says, "There is nothing here. Come on, let's move out."

⋏

I am not flailing in horror this time, as the memories from people's sufferings flood into my mind again. I know now this is exactly what these are, these are floods; the parable is clear to me. The visceral feeling of possessing the conscious thoughts of dying, crying, and of vulgarly brutal people all at once is no less consuming this time than the last. I simply am not flailing, because I am still undecided as to whether I can move at all or not.

I can vomit quite effectively though, and through my tears and the channeled cries of suffering souls, bile and whisky spill onto my lap. Climbing to my feet, as if having just lost a lengthy prize-fight, I gather my physical self together enough to walk; my spirit is still shaking the visions from its sight of the ruined baby girl. In my own memories I was just holding her shattered body in my hands, and I feel like I wish I had died too.

I know that I can die. I don't know why this occurs to me. But, whatever has happened, I have not been made immortal at all. It's just a simple shift in the mechanics that surround me, a fine tune made by the creator upon my earthly body. I can feel the second hand progressing still, as the mortal coil inside continues to unwind. Only now the tick is separated by long silences, and the sound of each movement echoes inside of me like dry thunder.

I stumble forward on my feet like a stand-in actor in a low budget zombie movie. Even across the distance, no greater than seventy feet, that I have careened, my stride begins to lengthen. By the time I reach the chain, now wearing a mangled dirt bike as a pendant, I'm able to smoothly step over with few residual grumblings. Walking back to the Humvee I stroll with what is almost a swagger, as I wonder to myself what other fun can be found in a bottle.

Looking into the backseat to ensure the girls are still tucked in, I actually feel awkward and embarrassed for my recent behavior. I smile at them reassuringly. "Dad has this under control, kids," I say to the aluminum tube in the back seat, more for my benefit than theirs.

The Humvee leaps to life when I engage the starter as if it, too, is ready to be getting onto a different scene. A quick inventory of my simple belongs confirms I am complete, and I pull out of the parking lot. No grand plan has been formed this morning. I'm feeling rather repentant and wish only to put the recent past behind me and allow the droning passage of miles under truck tires to provide a steady backdrop for some self- reflection.

I travel west through the town of Culpeper, where my father, grandfather, and great-grandfather had lived at various times. It's been over a year since I saw the sun setting over the Pacific Ocean. I now want only to put the past behind me, and to channel the Grateful Dead... head back to where the climate suits my clothes.

Back through the pastureland headed up to the Blue Ridge Mountains, I settle into my seat and focus only on the next turns, as they approach now in series. Concentrating on driving is preferred by me at this moment over giving the memories of the last several hours room to find an anchorage in my thoughts.

Approaching the entry to the Skyline Drive and the passage over the mountains, I see a small roadside vendor's stand. I pull over and gently break into the humble store. I grab a mason jar filled with apple butter and another containing raw honey and honeycomb. I'm still mildly hung over and pour the apple butter into my face like a teen-aged child; it is simply perfect. The honey I carry back to the Humvee and deposit into the messenger bag containing my Bible and my buds.

The big diesel engine creates an impressive display of noise and rich exhaust. It creates a far less impressive display of making rapid headway up the snaking road of Skyline Drive. I'm not interested in going quickly though, as the road is thickly littered with fallen limbs. More than a few cooler-sized boulders, which have dislodge from the hanging hillsides, prove effective to engage a wandering mind.

A bit more than halfway up to the crest formed by the Blue Ridge Mountains a small spring flowing directly from a stone hillside has been enshrined in large cut quarry stones. I stop the truck and set the brake, then walk over to investigate the springhouse.

A small stream of water escapes through what appears to be a solid piece of stone. Thickly matted algae grows at the apparent origin of the flow, and I press my puckered lips deeply into a soft mass that releases an ice-cold mouthful of clear water. I drink like this, kissing a hillside, until I rise back to my feet gasping for air.

I have no doubt whatsoever that this time, only months earlier, I would've just discovered a rapid weight loss program to envy any Hollywood insider. Now, with the adjustments to my earthly body, I know only that the numerous microbes I've just consumed will either play nicely with the fauna of my digestive track, or themselves be consumed for their nutrients. I walk to the truck and remove the jar of honey from the bag. Unscrewing the lid, I tilt the jar toward my open mouth and have a long, decadent, draw of thick sweetness.

I get the Humvee rolling again toward the point where I shall begin the downward grade into the Shenandoah Valley. Only minutes later I enter a short tunnel cut through a rocky point that the navigators of the Skyline's construction couldn't find a route around. I stop in the middle of the tunnel, the light from both ends barely reaching the point where I now sit.

I roll a cigarette from the bag of tobacco I'd lifted from the head shop. Stepping out into the cold, still air of the tunnel, the wetness here settles heavily upon me. I light the cigarette and climb onto the hood of the Humvee, sitting with my back against the windshield.

The quantity of alcohol I consumed the night before brought out the darker feelings building up inside of me: feelings of loneliness, incompletion, and a deep want for company. The dream of being sweetly sixteen had acted only as a harbinger to the onslaught of self-loathing it would herald into my waking mind. I am truly alone. And, while I've never minded my own company, I'm feeling rather pensive.

I look at my current placement, deep in a tunnel, with light in both directions. Coincidence is something I have always paid great attention to, as I've always felt it were a communication I could not quite comprehend. I have sought out this dark place on purpose, yet without conscious planning. I take a slow draw off the cigarette and close my eyes thinking of my feelings of isolation; the setting is blissful for dark introspection.

My mind steadies itself, my nose fills my lungs with cold, dank air, and my thoughts flow freely. Once again I think to myself as if gently lecturing. My own thoughts fill the positions of both master and apprentice, within the confines of my own mind. I reflect upon the light at the end of the tunnel, and in my imagination it represents love; my current place in the shadow becomes merely its absence.

I had read, while in the library of my winter retreat in Frenchtown, of this same internalized communication mentioned in the Bible. A friend had once called it, "the helper." It was not in a great wind, neither was it in an earthquake, or a fire, that the God of the Old Testament spoke. It was in a small voice. I had also read the instruction to "Be still and know that I am God."

I lie back and relax as if I'm about to catch a few winks. For the first time I notice the tinnitus in my ears, a remnant from teaching small arms in the Navy, is now gone. In this new silence, I find my voice speaking gently to me as if I'm whispering into both of my own ears at once; a brief mental picture flashes through my mind awkwardly, at best. This thought puts a smile on my face. I have no doubt that I'll remember what I heard myself thinking on my dying day just as well as when I first heard myself think it.

"The light of love can shine on nothing without also casting a shadow. Like the sun shining from above, through the leaves and limbs, of the mightiest tree, it too cast shadows onto the ground. These are not dark places; it is purely the mechanics of the physical world. It is then a choice of the witness who beholds this whether or not to linger in these cold shadows; it is by choice that one would not simply step into the light.

This is an ancient duality. It is natural and calm, only by our own invention is it ever a battle. There is no war being fought between a heaven and a hell. The light will always burn brightly. The light will always cast sharp shadows by contrast. The only battle is within our own intellect, and it is not one you can lose. The light was there before you; so shall it always be.

It is simply a choice. The only possible damnation into hell is your own decision. But it is a hell you can have no influence upon in the end. The release from your mortal bindings is already a certainty.

Your body will fold into the loam as readily as any leaf from a tree. The creation of infinity is not influenced either way. As I lay here, in an easy and casual trance, I feel myself lean in closer to my own ear. Speaking smoothly, through a smile, I listen as I say, 'Love is Light, Light is God, God is Love.' "

Thinking of the same words I'd seen carved into the lean-to the night of the Righting Moment, I say out loud, "Well, I do love coincidence, don't I?" I relight the cigarette, which has burned out without my attention, and taking a deep drag, I climb down from the Humvee's hood. I walk around and climb into the truck's cab and shut the door.

Leaning forward, rolled cigarette clenched in my teeth, I put my hand on the starter switch. I think of the words of the Buddha, "If you cannot find a good companion to walk with, walk alone, like an elephant roaming the jungle. It is better to be alone than to be with those who will hinder your progress."

The image of an elephant seems fitting enough, as moments later I come barreling out of the tunnel in a large, dirt-bathed behemoth of a truck. I squint as I reenter the bright sunshine of a clear spring afternoon, first looking to the Shenandoah River before me, and then simply west toward the horizon.

# Chapter 20

By evening I have managed to roll south through the Shenandoah Valley on I-81 passing over the James, then the New Rivers. Interstate 81 has always been one of my least favorite of the nation's interstates to travel on, simply due to the density of its truck traffic. However, as I now lumber along in a military vehicle it is appreciated, as the highway is a ready source of diesel fuel.

Already thick patches of weeds have found purchase in the growing cracks in the roads' surfaces. Large flakes of galvanizing have fallen from the guardrails. Rust is showing already, and I realize that in my life I will watch as all of this passes into oblivion.

The sun setting over the western sky is brilliant, as thick cumulous clouds light up from beneath like inverted alpenglow on a distant mountain range. Freshly refueled, the Humvee runs strong and clean. The lines flash by on the highway as barely adequate headlights cut into the growing darkness.

In a trance, free of thought, I barely notice the change in front of me in time. Skipping sideways, on four tires that bark as they skid, I come to an abrupt stop. The view from my passenger's door is completely obscured by a blue wall of steel. Climbing out of the truck as I casually roll another cigarette, I get out to investigate.

Fortunately the road has just changed from being divided by a wide median as it passes through a lazy S-turn. Had the road been flat and straight, my attention would have been too thin to react in time. Stepping around the front bumper of the truck, lighting my cigarette with closed eyes to preserve my vision, I open my eyes to miles of complete devastation.

A railroad bridge crosses over the highway here, and a train—obviously carrying something more potent than milk—has derailed and exploded. The highway signs overhead are melted and have hardened in strangely shining splatters on the road. I walk to the left to try to determine the scope of the carnage.

Less than one hundred yards through a small stand of trees, now simply blackened stakes rising from scorched earth, a driveway meets a small frontage road. A short distance ahead there is a large locomotive attached in tandem to another. Several of the leading cars lie tumbled atop the engines and, walking a bit further, I see three more locomotives have met from the opposing direction.

Retuning to the Humvee I backtrack to where the frontage road meets the highway and pull onto it. Soon I am forced off of the pavement and through an overgrown field, but the truck passes through without notice. Back onto the road I marvel at the magnitude of the accident. Only a few hundred yards before finally returning onto Interstate 40, in the whistle-stop of Silver Point, does the wreckage finally come to an end.

I drive another hour, maybe two, along the main highway and then pull over as I begin to grow suspicious of every shadow in my headlights. I am wearily tired from my alcohol-induced adventures of the recent past and decide to camp in the median of the highway. My simple tent and sleeping bag are familiar, and the comfort soon finds me asleep.

In the morning I wake up feeling very hungry, but opt to eat more highway miles as an appetizer before seeking out something more solid. I raise the large hood forward on the truck and make a quick inspection of the engine oil; it is low, and I'm glad I checked. I'll make certain to stop soon and replace the spent engine oil before I bring harm to my faithful steed through neglect.

Back in the saddle the miles again begin to disappear in the droning sound of the diesel pulling heavily lugged tires down the road. A quick glance to the paper road atlas and I determine it's best to skirt Nashville by taking the Briley Parkway. Twice I pass over the Cumberland River, stopping along the way to view the town center of Nashville.

The corporate center of the city stands at the water's edge with the river flowing by. During the minutes following the Righting Moment, a large jet – whether cargo or passenger I cannot tell— has dropped directly into the tallest section of the city. Much of the town center has been destroyed by what was obviously a powerful fire that followed as a result. With nobody left to contain the blaze, it'd moved freely between structures. The destruction is as impressive as it is horrible.

Shortly after the parkway rejoins the main interstate, passing endless layers of suburbia, I see a sign ahead for a large box-store retailer. I exit the highway here to seek out oil for the engine, food for myself, and it occurs to me an upgrade to my Humvee has also become unavoidable.

I grab the handle of a shopping cart as I cross the parking lot and push it to the entrance. As I approach, I see several of the front windows have been broken out by other carts. None are large enough to climb through without risking injury, though, so I decide to make my entrance the new-fashioned way. Spinning like a discus thrower, I lift the shopping cart and release it directly through the glass facade of the store; the resulting effects have never lost their appeal.

As I enter the store, an uncontrollable laugh erupts from me as a considerable band of raccoons hastily disappear into a nearby aisle and under tall display racks of clothing. The largest television figures on the air, before everything simply stopped, are now not only screen-printed onto dyed t-shirts, but are unwittingly harboring fugitive thieves. The fruits of these industrious intruders are apparent, as bags of white bread lie tossed about, and mixed with ripe feces. The white bread is apparently so enriched with chemicals, it appears still as edible as the day it was manufactured.

Walking toward the rear of the store, grabbing another shopping cart along the way, I see the dog and cat food aisle has previously hosted a sizeable party itself, as the amount of garbage is truly amazing. I smile, thinking how good it would be if I could only teach a raccoon to use a can opener. That chosen raccoon would then be worshipped by his kind, and be brought cans of cat food as homage by his masked minions while he reclined into a beanbag chair in home furnishings.

I place a compact disc car stereo and a set of enclosed speakers into the cart. I grab a collection of wiring looms, speaker wires, and a few simple tools to round out my order. On my way back to my vehicle, I toss in a can opener and a few cans of mixed vegetables to eat with a can of cold corned beef hash.

I mindlessly eat directly from the cans as I tie into the Humvees power feed and haphazardly install a stereo into the truck. Speaker wires and unused electrical leads combine on the floor of the passenger's side as if a spider with diarrhea has sneezed; this will do for now. The complete lack of craftsmanship will also wear on my sensitivities, and I know in time I'll have to readdress this installation.

I roll out of the parking lot to a nearby auto parts store as the Man in Black quotes Revelation 6:1, and then launches into, "The man comes around." The large diesel of the Humvee eats an impressive amount of engine oil before finally registering as being properly topped off. I throw a few gallon-sized bottles of coolant and some oil into the truck bed. Then I grab a foam pad to put on the driver's seat just for good measure.

I drain the belly tank of a parked delivery truck into the Humvee's fuel fill, and then am off to resume my drive westward. It is midday as I pass through the town center of Memphis. The time zone difference from the East Coast where I was when the Righting Moment occurred is obvious.

It was two o'clock in the morning, closing time at the bars, when the moment struck here. The clutter of cars, left abandoned, is much denser as a result; several times I am forced to find side streets to travel around piled-up vehicles. I make steady progress however, until the road before me simply comes to an end. I park a safe distance back and walk to the edge of the highway, which has collapsed into the Mississippi river.

It is immediately apparent what has happened. Several large composite tug-and-barges, along with a fully laden coastal freighter, have drifted against the spans of the bridge over the mighty Mississippi. With the personnel who were manning their helms gone, they had simply joined the energy of the river's flow, and come to be held against the bridge until it eventually failed.

Fortunately, an alternate route across the river is not far to the south. The bridge to Arkansas is still intact, and I cross without further delay. My progress is much more pleasant with music to keep me company. A music store in Little Rock was robbed by me; nobody seemed to notice. Classic rock plays through my open windows as I roll on down the highway.

I find myself on the open road again, after the mild inconvenience of more cluttered cars blocking smooth passage through Oklahoma City. Fueling stops at random tractor-trailers aside, the drive is all smooth sailing. I've just passed into Texas when I pull to a stop in the highway, kick my feet up onto the dash, and fall asleep with no fear of oncoming traffic.

# CHAPTER 21

I am back at the task of driving across the continent with the rising sun. Alongside the highway, I see a signpost advertising, "The best gun store in Texas." This is simply too bold of a statement to ignore, and I exit the highway. The scale of this store is amazing. Rather than being distracted by the vast array of weapons around me, however, my attention is instantly drawn to the first display case inside of the shattered front door.

Sitting on a mirror on top of it is a Barrett .50-caliber sniper rifle dressed out in a coyote- brown finish that matches my vehicle. An advanced military optical sighting system is mounted on top of its receiver. It is heavy and its potential energy is palpable as I lift it. That is that. In a record thirty seconds, my shopping is complete; the selection is final.

A brief search of the wildly overstocked ammunition section and I have four boxes of rounds for the weapon in hand. Each bullet looks more like the fid from a sailing ship's riggings than any round of ammunition I've ever fired outside of my time in the Navy. On ships, I'd fired a .50 caliber machine gun several times in training. This was to be a far more enjoyable experience, of that I had no doubt.

The store is located on a frontage road, in proper Southern style, and there is a stop sign approximately four hundred yard away. I load three rounds into the magazine and, putting the bi-pod back into use, I assume a prone position and center the sight onto the stop sign. The report is a shock, the sear breaks free, and the round goes off far sooner than expected.

I regain my composure and release the last two rounds toward the stop sign as well. A short walk confirms the need to adjust the sights.

A little bit of tinkering later, I roll right through an intersection and past a stop sign with six holes in the letter O. I've strapped the Barrett into the seat opposite of the girls and placed the magazine loaded with only three rounds into the messenger bag. This bag is soon due for an upgrade, I think, as I look at a simple leather one on the floor.

"This neighborhood is going downhill, Morrison," I say to myself. Then I add over my shoulder to my daughters, "When we get to California, girls, I'm taking you for a ride in a Bentley."

The climate here feels like a different planet to me; the land-scape adds to the effect. Texas slides quietly into New Mexico with no more fanfare than a simple sign. My mind cannot help but wander as I scan the landscape of the countryside that surrounds me. The land itself is powerful, humbling, the openness of the space feels as if it expands inside of me. You would think that be-ing surrounded by so much open "nothingness" would make me feel insignificant; its effect is just the opposite.

Halfway to Albuquerque I stop in Santa Rosa, a small town that the interstate actually was built to curve right around. The area feels disproportionately rich with lush vegetation, as if the rain that avoids the surrounding lands falls freely here. I walk into a small general store and pocket a disposable lighter on my way past the register. A can of baked beans and a spoon from the condiment bar and I get back into the truck and onto the highway.

There's a road sign that says "Blue Hole." Not terribly exciting, but enough to get me to turn both my attention, and the truck, to see a blue hole. I try to put my sailor's mind to use coming up with something inappropriate; surprisingly I come up with nothing.

As it turns out this was a perfect decision as the blue hole is an azul-colored sinkhole filled with cool, clean water, and it appears to be a giant artesian well. I strip naked and dive into the water and float neutrally suspended in this oasis abyss for several minutes before leisurely pulling to the surface. I lie peacefully on my back under a sky that is filled with bright sun shining down on me, even as a large thunderhead is developing to the west.

Walking back to the truck, my clothes hanging over one arm, I wear nothing but my boots. I drive to the first house I see, break in, and find a towel in a hallway closet. The idea of searching for clean clothes passes my mind, instead I line the truck seat with the towel and sit as naked as the day I was born only wearing boots.

It's a short drive until I'm entering Albuquerque, and as I come into town I see a sign for a local high school. On the sign is a banner for a book drive supporting their expanded library. A good book to read as I pass my evenings sounds like a great idea; I again take a short diversion from my mission to reach the Pacific coast.

# Chapter 22

The desert air smells heavily of ozone from approaching rains. The sky is heavy, like molten lead rolling in slowly from the west. A storm is coming, and I eagerly await it. I have always marveled at the power and majesty of a good thunderstorm.

I pull into the parking lot of the school feeling somewhat vulnerable because of my nakedness. The ridiculousness of this is only beginning to dawn on me when I hear something out of place... hard breathing, labored and panicked. The sound of a mortal struggle fills my blood with rising energy, even as I work out where its source is originating.

It's coming from a large facility opposite the main school buildings across the same parking lot; a sign on the building shows that it's a swimming pool. The struggle sounds desperate, and fully engaged. My first thought is that people are fighting, whether in anger or not I can't tell. I pull my deer rifle out of the truck and sprint off across the parking lot toward the sounds.

A large tree has fallen, I would imagine by a violent windstorm in the past, and has smashed its breaking limbs against the building's side. Glass has been shattered and large openings expose the scene inside. There is a mature cow elk fighting to get free from the pool. A thick plastic covering had been rolled onto the waters surface; the animal is exacerbating its situation in a blind panic.

I walk to the edge of the pool to try to determine a course of action to help save the distressed animal. It's obvious that she wandered in at some point, and her senses hadn't established the surface as a hazard until it was too late. Now, in a wild-eyed fury she struggles and is only pulling the cover more tightly around her flailing body.

Out of instinct I reach to my waist for my knife before re-membering my current clothing selection is completely without belt loops, let alone a knife. I bend over, and taking off my boots, dive in to try to free the struggling beast. The water is a full twelve feet deep here, and I tread in a section where the plastic has been pulled away by the elk.

The very water of the pool telegraphs an instant sense of dread into my body. The piston-like cycling of the beast's front legs pushes concussive waves through the fluid surrounding me, and the pulse of it is physically disturbing. The sheer volume of the breath being labored by the elk's powerful muscles is blurred into static when combined with the bombastic splashing of its hooves. The entirety of this animals struggle makes logical thought hide behind a mammalian instinct to flee.

I gather together a large collection of the plastic covering, making certain I gather equally from each side of the wallowing cow. With the cover firmly captured in the crook of my bent arm, I begin an inverted scissor kick in an effort to tow the creature to the water's edge.

I focus on the side of the pool and reach forward drawing strongly in a sidestroke motion. As I begin to feel the slightest progress, a hammering blow comes down on my right femur. The large nerve, which runs down the side of the thigh, the common peroneal, sends a dizzying stun into my mind. Out of sheer instinct my body doubles to protect itself, even as a second sledgehammer lands into my ribs beneath my armpit, knocking the air from my lungs.

I'm already deeply winded from exertion and out of breath. The release from this moments panic is not to be found, however, as my head rises up into the thick plastic and I'm pulled into the maelstrom of turning hooves.

The abuse is complete; it's as if the panic-blinded beast is trying to climb onto my back to find higher ground. Through sheer luck the noose slips from around my neck and, in a brief flash of thoughtfulness, I pull hard for the bottom of the pool. My lungs, already on fire, are trying desperately to trick my diaphragm to gasp for air.

I swim beneath the drowning elk and rise against the pool cover. I see a small bubble of air, no larger than a soccer ball, and try to siphon it in through puckered lips. The effort is a monumental failure as water rushes into my mouth and gags me as it attempts to seek entry into my lungs.

I turn my vision and see the bright section of open water. Kicking feverishly, dragging myself hand over hand, I make a mindless race toward the air it illuminates. I burst through the water's surface. Hanging on the side of the pool by my armpits, I take in large gulps of air; it is sweeter than any wine.

I climb out and slide onto my belly before rolling onto my back. Each breath I draw brings sharp and heavy pain into my chest. I can feel a deep contusion just below my right armpit, although moving doesn't seem to indicate any broken ribs. My right thigh already looks as if I've been powerfully struck by two blows from a teardrop-shaped hammerhead, or perhaps by a drowning elk's hoof.

Rising to my feet, I immediately meet the direct gaze of the despair in the failing creature's gaze. Its muzzle is dripping with mucus, a thin line of blood runs out of one nostril, and its eyes are widely framed in white. There is simply no way this will end well for her.

I pick up the rifle from the tiled floor where I'd dropped it when I came in. I pull the bolt back slightly to ensure there is, in fact, a round in the chamber. I then walk to the edge of the pool nearest the elk. Already the pace of its struggle has slowed, and it now battles just to keep its face above the surface.

I tell her, "Everyone deserves to hear this in the end, old girl... I love you."

I focus on a spot just beneath her ear and let the round go loose from the rifle. The spent animal slips into a closing blue grave of plastic sheeting as deep red blood turns its surface in an expansion of bright royal purple.

I can't say exactly why, but I do something I haven't felt the urge to do in quite some time: I sit on the ground and I cry. The release brings with it the opening of other floodgates. I cry for my children, I cry for my friends, I cry for the world I miss with all of my heart. I cry for my life as it once was, and then I cry some more.

My rifle slung over my shoulder, I walk out of the pool facility and back into the world. The sky has grown darker, and a powerful storm is approaching quickly. My head is heavy; the killing of the female elk is disproportionately breaking my heart. I walk by the Humvee, tossing my rifle into passenger's side. I roll up all of the windows and head into the high school. I enter through a rear door, at the end of a long aluminum awning, and kick aside freshly broken glass.

A long hall of locker-lined walls stretches out before me. Looking through closed classroom doors, I see everything as it had been years ago. I, too, had once sat in a plastic chair with a desktop similar to the ones inside. With the exception of installed flat screens on the walls, taking the place of monolithic tubed televisions on tall rolling carts, the image is complete for me, down to old glory hanging proudly in the front of each room.

Where the hall meets at a junction with a wider hall, I turn toward what will surely be the administrative heart of the deserted school, and from there I can intuitively find the library. Near the front of the building I see a sign for the dispensary, although nobody had ever called it anything other than the nurse's office. Perhaps in the name of force-fed equality they'd replaced the sign to reflect a more neutral impression.

I step into the nurse's office to see what supplies I may find useful, expecting little beyond the most pedestrian of items. In a small room to the rear there is a single steel bed, the crisp white sheet upon it still tightly bound to the mattress with sterile looking hospital corners. Absent-mindedly, I pull the sheet off of the bed and tuck it as a bundle under my left arm.

On the table next to the two steel and plastic chairs that comprise the waiting area, I see a large black permanent marker. I pick it up and walk out of the dispensary, through the display case lined vestibule, and out the main entrance of the school. The sky is ominous, and the air ripe with the smell of the incoming weather.

I walk to the flagpole in the center of a large turning basin meant for the handling of busloads of students. There's a cast cement pad on the ground before the flagstaff. The halyards are neatly bound to a cleat in tight figure eights. I drop to my hands and knees on the cement and lay the sheet out flat on the ground before me.

Pulling the cap off of the marker with my teeth and then spitting it out of the way, I write my name on the top of the sheet in bold block-styled letters. Not even certain of why, I ask, "What am I doing? What do I want?" Then, without hesitation I begin to answer myself.

In neat letters, with the pungent smell of the marker filling the air, I write what I want. "I want my children back." "I want a home filled with laughter." "I want a partner who simply trusts me because they know me." "I want the world back as it was." "I want to find a good job, one I love." "I want the arms of a lover." Even as I write, my hand begins moving more sloppily.

I grow more urgent in my wanting, more personal, more honest. "I want people to see me as successful." "I want people to envy my appearance." "I want to have influence over people." "I want to have money to travel." "I want people to see my success and notice me, call me great." I pour out my laundry list of desires one after the other.

Having nobody to judge me, no one to look over my shoulder, I pull out deeper from inside of my own ego. "I wish I were taller, thinner framed." "I wish my penis were larger." "I wish I had never stolen from friends." "I wish I had applied myself more at everything I had done." "I wish I had forgiven more easily, and judged less often."

My handwriting has grown into a random scrawl; my eyes are dropping large tears onto the sheet blurring written lines of ink. I fill the entire page with what I want for me. I end my manically written manifesto of selfishness with, "I want to be loved."

Then, turning the pen in my hand I drive the frayed felt tip into the sheet with full force, and carve the letter "I" into the fabric darkly. Tossing the marker aside and looking across my written words, I feel broken of these wants even as I have written them.

I reach to the edge of the cement pad and gather two large pieces of gravel into my hand. I rise to my feet, picking up the sheet with me. Folding the sheet under my arm, I undo the figure eights holding the halyard in place on the flagstaff.

By folding two corners of the fabric over each piece of gravel, I jam the halyard clips to the sheet and raise my flag slowly to the truck atop the flagstaff. Pulling the slack tightly from the halyard I bend the line back around the cleat. Then I step back to observe my deepest desires as they fly full of pride in the growing wind.

I'm drawn to a movement a short distance away. A mockingbird has landed. He hops a few times and then suddenly spreads his wings. He then turns his head sharply and watches for an instant before hopping again, repeating the gesture. It occurs to me exactly what he is doing. The bird is making his shadow cast out before him and triggering insects to respond to the change in their environment. By doing this he can trick them into giving away their position.

As I watch, the bird darts his head forward and plucks from the ground a shiny black cricket. Satisfied, he flies off. The white bars on his wings make me think of the invasion stripes of a P-51 Mustang, flying off to hunt more targets of opportunity. The bird, I realize, wants nothing. It is just a bird; its needs are met, and it has no desire but to continue to live.

The trees across the once-mowed lawns before me begin to sway as the wind builds. Green leaves take to the air, released by the invisible pull of the rising storm's grip. The first sheet of rain rolls across the ground, advancing on me quickly; a chill raises goose bumps on my naked flesh. The rain does not build... it simply falls. The ground is saturated in an instant, and the large raindrops hit leaving small craters in the standing water like meteorite impacts.

I step back onto the cement pad. Looking up to the flag of my own ego, I drop to the ground on my knees. With both hands

I pull my hair back and away from my face. I put my hands on the heels of my ankles and sit back upon them. The heavy raindrops fall onto my face with brief stinging shocks.

The first bolt of lighting lands in the grassy field before me. I've seen lightning strike this closely into open ocean water before. In the sea, it formed an illuminated loom of a peculiar greenish blue, not unlike the color of the love of my daughters. Here, on open ground, the energy rips through the air as intense light, a physical wall of noise, as one would certainly expect. However, there is a taste in my mouth like I've bitten a handful of tinfoil, and the hairs on my entire body stand erect.

I look up to the ego flag, and it has collapsed around the flag-staff. One of the jammed cleats has broken loose, the halyard clip ringing the hollow metal tube of the flagpole with a cadence that is like an advancing German Army. I await the next bolt of lightning to hit the pole and complete the magical quickening I anticipate.

The lightning, however, never strikes nearby again. The storm is releasing its fury upon the land behind me even now. I can count between the flashes of light, and the thunder that follows only a brief second. But I feel the charged air in the storm diminishing quickly. The rain shows no such interest in retreating.

I rise and walk to the flagpole and release the halyard, slowly peeling the flag from its constrictor-like hold, and hoping the last clip holding it does not slip as well. I bring the flag down into my hands and release the clip that has held it aloft. The rain has soaked the words together and suspended the ink in the water-logged fabric.

I stroll across the field toward the nearby tree line. As I walk, I find opposite corners of the sheet with each hand. I loft the wet sheet heavily into the air above me, and it falls back down across my arms and shoulders like a mold of wet plaster. I stand with my back to the trees with my arms stretched out to my sides widely. I look up to the falling sky and say, "Thank you!"

The ink-filled water from the sheet releases all of my wants across my skin. The black stain flows down my naked flesh slowly, following the deep contours of my muscles, forming small eddies around each hair as it passes. I simply stare into the falling rain unblinking as all of my desires flow over me and melt away like tattoos exposed to a crematorium's infernal flames.

I am absolutely unchanged; my heart beats without effort, my eyes see without training, and my soul loves without expectation. I am unchanged, yet completely altered as the last of my desires rolls across the tops of my feet and vanishes between the tall grasses.

A movement flashes through the corner of my vision, and I whip my head around to meet it. The mockingbird lights onto a low limb in a nearby tree to find shelter from the torrential rain. My gaze falls squarely onto the unassuming gray creature. I see only a bird. The bird's black bead of an eye looks to me too and sees only a man.

# Chapter 23

There is a man striding powerfully across a parking lot, empty save for a military utility vehicle. The wet blacktop beneath his feet reflects the first rays of sunlight breaking through thinning clouds, which pass by quickly overhead. He is naked, his lean body moves like an animal's.

He is wildly alert, scanning purposefully, yet without the goals of the agendas he'd once pursued. Reaching inside of the truck he slides on a pair of weathered pants, then laces heavy leather boots onto bare feet. Scanning his back trail one last time, he steps into the truck and drives off.

He doesn't know what day of the week it is, or what week of what month it is. He knows only that he needs to keep moving. Although, even of why that is, he doesn't bother to question. He knows only that he is thankful that he is alive. He needs to do nothing to simply be thankful, so that's what he chooses to be.

Following the street that the school was on he heads west through deserted rows of hastily built homes, each one more alike than the last. Looking past these useless structures he lets his vision linger on the mountains that form the skyline to the north. Slowing to go over the curb, riding easily up a cement embankment, then easing back onto the road, he maneuvers around a mass transit bus that is blocking the exit onto Route 85.

Picking up a good head of steam down an empty onramp, with the big diesel pulling the truck powerfully, he reaches over and hits play on the truck's stereo. The Man in Black plays a driving guitar riff and sings a remake about someone to hear your prayers. A small wake of vultures scatters from picking over a large hare as the truck muscles noisily past. The hare chose, he notes with an easy smile, a most ironic location to choose to die of natural causes.

Taking a break, after siphoning a tank of fuel from an abandoned truck, he stands on the steel guardrail and settles deeply onto his own heels. Finishing the cigarette he had rolled, then flicking it's spent butt onto the dusty road, he looks again to the mountains to his north. The mountains are not grand as far as the scale of mountains goes. Still, his gaze lingers as if he is looking for something.

Like a teenaged child would've stood before an open refrigerator before their attention turns elsewhere, he, too, decides there is nothing that holds his interest after all. Walking back to the truck, he reaches over and pulls the aluminum tube holding his children free from their safety restraint. He lovingly places them onto the oversized center console and says, "You guys ride up here with me for a while. The scenery is changing, and I want you to see it all."

In less than an hour, he has passed Santa Fe. A short while later, he sees a road sign indicating Las Vegas is soon approaching. His mind turns over this apparent mistake of geography until he sees Las Vegas, New Mexico. Without the slightest urge to exit the highway he notes to himself that this must, in fact, be quite a different city than the one named for sin. The mountains remain, for the most part, hovering outside of his side window. He feels a pull to head toward these nearby hills. The question of why never crosses his mind.

Again the terrain outside of the truck makes a slow and subtle shift, and soon he recognizes his entire surroundings have changed. Long hills rise easily, rolling into one another like gentle waves. Tall wild grasses grow thickly on the hillsides, backlit strongly by the sun; they glow with a rich vitality. The highway ahead goes over a small bridge as it crosses over a smaller highway, marked as 120.

For a moment he studies the linked cars of a train, which has expired along the roadside to his right. Then his attention is caught by a herd of cattle grazing on a lush hillside in the near distance across the other side of the road. Even as he is processing the anomaly of seeing cows for the first time in so very long, he is slowing and allows the truck to coast over the berm of the highway.

The truck settles to a stop in the shade of a small overpass. He reaches down onto the dash and puts the engine to sleep. Exiting the truck, leaving the door open behind him, he walks to where he can get a clear view of the cattle. The instant the first one comes into view, he sees the mystery has been replaced by wonder.

On a hillside, grazing freely and wildly beneath a bright blue sky, there is a herd of perhaps sixty bison. He stands, arms crossed on his chest, taking in the most amazing sight he's witnessed since meeting his first child. How could this have come to pass in such a short period of time? What has it been... seven, eight months at the most? He decides these must have been farmed animals, kept for their lean and expensive flesh, which had slipped the boundaries of the ranch where they were raised.

Yet, still, the sight of wild buffalo roaming this green plain between ranges of ruggedly beautiful mountains is a powerful one. He admires the beasts as they move together slowly down the ridgeline less than a thousand yards away. The elk he'd killed in the pool had been too emotional of an event for him stop and take sustenance from the stricken animal; emotions he is not currently encumbered by.

He glances at the buffalo over his shoulder as he begins walking quickly back to the truck and says, "Thank you for this bounty you have laid before me." Reaching in through the passenger door, he pockets the magazine of .50 caliber rounds. Then grabbing the Barrett by the barrel and hefting it onto his shoulder he adds, "Amen."

Climbing up through an opening between the two lanes of traffic above, he takes an elevated position that provides him with a clear line of sight to the buffalo. Opening the bipod, he assumes a prone position on the hot road surface. He pulls the charging handle on the receiver to the rear, and releases a round of into the rifle's chamber.

He places his forehead onto his left arm and closes his eyes. Breathing slowly, smoothly, he allows all tension to flow out through his nose. His body settles downward, physical tension floods out as if pulled by Earth's gravity itself. He raises his head easily allowing his cheek to find purchase on the rifle's stock.

He keeps both eyes open; the muscles associated with closing only one strains the other. Shifting the rifle tighter into himself while bringing the animals into focus, he begins to visually cull through the herd. One of the larger bison is standing a bit aloofly. Any young ones do not accompany it, and it moves differently in a subtle manner; it is tired.

He reaches out to it in his thoughts. He apologizes for taking its life to sustain his own. He promises to show it loving respect, to take its life well.

The distance to the animals is not far for the rifle he is brandishing. The round of ammunition fired by this weapon can effectively kill at several times this range. Yet the shot will require his full ability to be perfect. Seven hundred yards can multiply the slightest error tremendously.

He focuses on the animal's side, forward of its center and into a pocket where its shoulder joins its ribs. He knows well the structure of a large mammal and intends to put a round through both of its lungs, with its heart being shattered between them. As he once heard a Master Chief he'd bow hunted with say, "A torpedo through the boiler room."

As he places his finger onto the trigger and begins to conceive the shot to follow, there is a shift in the mood of the herd. Several animals' heads turn to look behind them; animals in the front seem to become wary of their surroundings as well. He takes his finger from the trigger and scans the surrounding hillside through the powerful optics atop the rifle.

There is a stand of trees on the crest of the hill the bison have been grazing upon. He sees a movement in the tall grass between the trees and vectors his full attention upon it. What appears to be a small mound of exposed earth, like an ant mound, is visible and he watches it intently. Ant mounds may have a nasty habit of appearing out of nowhere, but they do not move. This one does.

Suddenly, a lone wolf erupts from the tall grass, instantly in full stride toward the herded animals. Two other wolves join into the charge, the ant mound being one of them. Raising his head to watch through his own eyes rather than through the narrow confined view of the scope, he sees several other wolves have launched their attack simultaneously from over the ridgeline on the opposite side of the herd.

First seeing the pack of wolves before them, the bison turn in unison and begin to retreat. The animals on the uphill side instantly plant their hooves in protest as they spot the advancing attack party of wolves closing the distance from above. The entire herd stacks up tightly upon itself before being forced to run instead across the sloped meadow.

One of the wolves from the uphill group has already closed the gap and launches into the rear flank of a large bison at the rear of the group. Quickly other wolves have joined into the assault on this isolated animal. The herd has stopped. Several of the bison have already begun to turn back into the pack of wolves like furry locomotives that have jumped their tracks.

The counterattacking beasts run right through the pack of wolves. One lowers its head and plows powerfully into a wolf; the wild dog is sent skyward. Even as the wolf is in midair, its back braces itself and its legs extend to the rear, effectively catching its fall. The wolf stands in defiance, apparently unscathed from the wrecking ball's blow.

All the while the other wolves are distracting, molesting the separated bison. Powerful bites are being landed upon it from several directions at once. The attack ends only as the herd returns to envelope the wounded bison in the safety of its sheer mass. The wolves back away but remain closely engaged, snapping at the outer animals in the herd; their snarls and barks fill the air with palpable tension.

The man on the bridge focuses once more through the rifle's powerful scope, quickly finding the injured bison. Its chest is heaving to pull in air. The muzzle of the bison is draining mucus in a thick bubbling flow. Wild eyes show pain and panic alike. The beast is unsteady; the herd is unsteady as well.

As he looks across the distance between himself and the injured animal thin lines distort the air between them, visible only through the magnification of the scope. Like salt being dissolved into clean water, this rising thermal moves slowly from the right to the left.

He knows that this movement will affect the bullet he releases. He adjusts not only for the fall of the bullet's trajectory, but allows also for the drift to the left. He chooses one dot from the many on the scope's reticle to become the revised point of impact. He sights once more into the chest of the struggling bison.

He waits patiently, knowing the round will pass through the animal with enough energy to do collateral damage to anything beyond his intended target. He is looking for a break in the animals behind the heaving bison. He begins to slowly apply pressure to the trigger without consciously focusing on the movement. An opening appears in the space to the rear of the bison, and the powerful rifle rips through the afternoon's air with thunderous effect.

Through the magnified image provided through the scope, he sees the path of the bullet. It appears as if a wormhole boring through the sheer illusion of reality itself. Like a ripple in still water, it floats upon the rising thermals and does, indeed, drift slowly to the left.

The blow strikes the struggling bison directly into what would be its armpit, had it arms. Energy expands across the side of the animal as if watching the concussion of an exploding bomb dropped from a plane in an old war movie. The animal simply drops. It raises its head once in protest as thick blood escapes from its open mouth, then it is finished.

The man stands and gathers the large rifle into his arms, cradling it as he runs, and he returns to the truck beneath the bridge. He quickly renders the rifle inert by removing the magazine and ejecting the round from its chamber. He discards the magazine and loose round into the messenger bag on the floor of the truck. Placing the rifle into the passenger's side as well, he circles the truck and gets inside, starting it before even closing the door fully.

The Humvee barrels out of the shadows from beneath the bridge with a wide-open throttle. A thin line of dark gray smoke streams out of its exhaust. As he closes the distance on the fallen bison, the wolves have already disappeared from view.

He comes to a stop only thirty feet from the bison. Before he even exits the vehicle he is struck by the majestic stature of the beast. Even as it lays in death, its presence is a powerful one. He steps out of the truck and walks to the slain animal. He kneels beside its head as it stares vacantly off into infinity. The man places his hand over the large eye and pulls its eyelid shut with a smooth and gentle caress.

"You went easily, old girl," he says. "I will take only what I need and leave the rest to those wolves who need you too. Thank you for what you are providing for us."

He pulls the knife from its sheath on his hip. This knife had felt so capable kneeling over a whitetail deer. Now in his hand he feels as if he has a plastic sword designed for the task of putting an olive to its grave. He steps around the animal to the small of its back; his intention is to open a section of its hide, peel back the skin, and simply remove a large section of the loin.

He pushes hard to insert the knife through the dense hide with the blade pointed upwards, rather than downward, in order to use the energy of the first cut to begin a long and rough incision. The knife hesitates until the blade opens an entry perhaps three inches long. Instinctively he stops and turns quickly on his heels.

Two of the wolves are standing less than eighty feet away; their strong bodies lowered and ready to charge. He looks to his left and sees three more coming up the hill already in full stride. Without formulating a plan, or giving it a single thought, he is stepping on, and then over the fallen bison, in a blind dash for the safety of his truck.

Even as he safely jumps into the driver's side seat, a large wolf lands on the hood from a third direction and leaps through the space he'd filled only a heartbeat earlier. He slams the door behind him as the wolf, having pivoted instantly upon landing, leaps its front paws against the thin section of glass, helping him ensure the door is fully latched.

The wolf steps down and walks only feet away and turns to look squarely into the man's eyes. The romanticized notions of those he'd known before the Righting Moment would believe there to be some kindred spirit between a man and a wolf. The wolf, he is completely aware, is without any such misgivings of feeling brotherly love toward any man.

The wolf's posture actually becomes more threatening than it had been when it'd intended to kill the man. Launching into the pack of wolves, it chases every other one away from the kill with its presence alone. It walks to the front of the bison and, with a powerful bite and single brutal pull, removes a large section of its muzzle.

The man sits in the truck for a moment watching. His body is still flooded with the hormones of panic, which had saved his life. Under his breath he says, "You guys actually had me triangulated. I am humbled by your skill. Had you taken me it would have been a good death you gave me."

With wildly shaking hands, he rolls the worst cigarette possibly ever rolled. But only after liberally garnishing his lap with spilled loose tobacco and wasting three rolling papers in the process. He lowers his window and allows his body to regain its natural rhythm, smoking deep pulls into his lungs, and noting with disdain that the world's tobacco supply has officially gone stale.

The man starts the Humvee; the wolves take notice but do not give up their ground. He turns around slowly in the tall grass and follows his own trail back down the hill.

He mutters to himself, "Welcome back to the food chain, Morrison." Driving under the overpass, he enters the town of Wagon Mound and comes across a street sign for Long Street. The name is a bit of an exaggeration, however, as after driving only three short blocks he reaches the end of the road. A brief trip through the desolate neighborhood and he comes across what appears to be the only grocery store in town.

The door is heavily barred shut. In fact, much of the area shows a disproportionate amount of security in place. It's almost as though the sheer depression of this place must've led to a downward spiral of poverty and the problems that always used to accompany desperation. The barred door gives almost no protest as it is winched from the building. He winds the synthetic cable back into the winch on the front of the truck before entering the store.

He'd been visualizing lean cuts of bison filet smoking over an open campfire in his mind before the wolves took that fantasy away. Canned tamales, a can of mustard greens, and three cans of Vienna sausages are rounded up instead to make a paltry replacement meal. He explores unrefrigerated bottles of water. They seem to be generally benign, and he leaves three empty bottles on the floor.

On his way back to the entrance, he sees a small glass display case under the cash register. Inside there is a collection of novelty knives for sale. Beside them is a row of Japanese throwing stars.

Reaching to the end of a nearby aisle, he grabs a can of dog food and casually pitches it through the glass cabinet.

He's never used a throwing star, and the idea seems to tickle his fancy. So he pushes aside a large piece of broken glass and picks one out from the others. The throwing star is matte black and has the word "Ninja" printed in white letters on its side. He looks toward the door and sees what had served as a community bulletin board and hurls his ninja star at it playfully, but with earnest effort.

He rounds up his canned food goods and walks toward the door, stopping to see how deeply the throwing star had entered the corkboard. The star has stuck squarely into the middle of a printed flyer for the Bandelier National Monument. The top of the column it has been thumbtacked to reads, "Things to do in Wagon Mount."

He pulls the throwing star out of the bulletin board and drops it to the floor. Then he pulls the pamphlet from the bulletin board as well. A brief scan of the map on the back shows that things to do in town are apparently only a two and a half hour drive away.

Amused by the abundance of local attractions, he looks on and sees a picture of a Cliffside once inhabited by the Pueblo tribe and is now a sightseeing destination. On the second page there is a glossy image of a place called the Alcove house. In the picture it shows several large ladders that must be climbed to reach it.

The Cliffside dwellings of the Pueblo have always held a certain allure to him. Earlier, while traveling along the highway, he'd felt a strong draw to these very mountains. Once he might've said, "I have to go there."

Now, he simply knows it is where he is going.

# CHAPTER 24

The drive back to Santa Fe is slowed only by the need once more to feed his persistently hungry truck. Another of the ever-present deserted big rigs serves the only purpose it will ever know again. Turning north on Route 84 into town, he is struck by the image of the waxing gibbous moon hanging over the city. The mountains beyond, which are soaking in a bright purple alpenglow, frame the city's skyline.

There is an exit sign marking the way toward a canyon road off to his right. The shadows are growing long anyway; if he stops here for the night, he'll be well placed to get to the Bandelier in the morning. He follows the roads by the direction they travel rather than any particular destination. At one point his progress is thwarted as he winds up dead ended in a development of large and identical builder homes; each with the quasi- styling that self-defines the Midwest.

He stops in front of a row of houses that would've been particularly expensive in their time. Little flags, only beginning to sun fade, show their inhabitants had lived behind key pads and panic buttons. He only has to search two before finding exactly what he's looking for.

In an unlocked box, under a stack of brand new dress shirts, on the top shelf of a bedroom, he pulls it out and inspects his prize. A stainless steel .44 magnum revolver thoughtfully left for him in a well-tooled leather holster. He undoes his belt and removes the knife, sliding the holster on his right hip. The knife is placed forward by one belt loop, then he hitches his pants back onto his hips comfortably.

He walks over to a tall dresser and, under a neatly lined row of rolled dress socks, he finds a box of hollow-point cartridges for the weapon. He swings open the cylinder and easily slides one shell into each of the six bores that await them. He pushes the cylinder back into the pistol's frame.

Extending the pistol out at arm's length, he sights on himself in a tall vanity mirror. Not from fear of seven years bad luck, rather preferring not to watch himself shoot himself, he adjusts slightly to the right and drops the pistol's sights onto an unsuspecting clock radio.

He squeezes the trigger, then realizing the weapon is single action, thumb cocks the hammer and squeezes again; the room is filled with a roar as the heavy bullet sends the idling clock radio into many directions at once before vanishing into the sheetrocked wall. Without bothering to replace the spent cartridge, he slides the pistol into his holster and fixes it in place with a simple leather loop over the hammer.

Looking again at his image in the mirror he says, "Is that you John Wayne?" Standing there regarding himself, with no eye toward scrutiny, he takes simple stock of the man he has become. He wouldn't have recognized himself if this man had walked by him on the Appalachian Trail.

His torso is tightly muscled, ribs extend out between the marked cuts between them, his shoulders are balled with corded muscles, and long hair falls easily past his shoulders. His beard has grown to the length of his collarbone. His eyes simply observe with the vacant interest that a housecat may give to a painting.

Driving out of the development, he navigates his way through completely barren roads that were once lined heavily with suburban sprawl. As he drives higher, outside of the city limits, he comes to a pull off that provides a wide panoramic view of the darkened city below. The moon hangs heavily just above the mountains beyond; its bright light uninterrupted by any clouds in the sky.

Once, in youthful feelings of longing confused with love, he'd spoken to a girl offering reassurance to one another of their proximity always as they stood under this same moon. He can deeply identify with the feeling, although it no longer has any gravity to pull at the strings in his heart. In his life before the Righting Moment he had come to know only one true love. A love he'd neglected, and then lost.

Standing, still shirtless, the man feels no longing for that love anymore. He is certain only that she, too, felt the pain of its absence. However, he couldn't find the remorse in himself, which had once driven like a fist into his own gut. He had simply been who he was, a man deeply unfinished; his now dead ego had betrayed him more than any lover ever had. With this simple truth, his forgiveness of himself is complete.

Pulling his sleeping bag from the truck, he places it onto a thick growth of grass that has found purchase beside the pavement of the pull off. First untying, then removing his boots, he removes his pants and stands fully exposed to the world. He slides into the sleeping bag, and then unzips it halfway to his waist. He folds his hands behind his head and looks up into a sky filled with clouds of stars.

ANDREW S FINCHAM

Without a single ambient light in the world, except perhaps for a firefly a few hundred miles away, the night sky is in its full glory. Constellations of far away stars act out tales of their own invention. Without an audience to define them, the freedom to shine is only amplified. He lies there looking up into the very engine of eternity.

Before closing his eyes to sleep he says, "I had never known happiness because I pursued it too hard. There is nothing in creation that does not grow more distant with the force of a push. I am whole now, even if alone, and my love has finally slipped free from its reigns. Thank you."

He watches the sky for a moment, half expecting some shooting star to close his simple prayer with confirmation. Then he realizes that the confirmation was in hearing his own words. He closes his eyes, and sleep takes him into its accepting arms without pause.

The morning comes without fanfare. The ridge to his right is just barely visible from the rising sun. He stretches himself in a long, circular bend from the waist, and then puts on his clothes. Ensuring the pistol is firmly held fast in it's holster, he enters his truck and wonders if, perhaps, he can find a sealed bag of fresh coffee anywhere in the world still. He may not have the same wants that had once served as blind static to the truths of his own life, but he desires a good cup of coffee nonetheless.

Driving with a purpose, growing yet still undefined, he winds the heavy truck back down the narrow twisting road. Back onto the highway, he pushes his faithful diesel powered steed into a gallop. The pamphlet's map guides him to a road labeled as 502.

The sign reads that it leads to Los Alamos. He halfheartedly thinks to himself that it may be rather fun to explore the elusive secrets of the installations of that once forbidden location. To be free to explore what truths are to be discovered— truths that were once so mysteriously steeped in urban-legend.

He does not have a bucket list. The thought falls instead into a file waiting in his mind. A thought with a bright plastic tab stuck to it for later indexing that has the words, "may be interesting" handwritten upon it in blue ink.

Violating several laws regarding the safe operation of a motor vehicle, he bounds across oncoming lanes and grass medians alike. His barking tires announce his arrival onto Route 4, and then he hammers on southbound. He rolls powerfully past a bedroom community called White Rock.

His gallop finally slows to an easy trot as the road is forced into tightening switchbacks. The edge of the pavement offers no buffering zone of forgiveness; it drops off precipitously into steep cliffs. He stops once in the middle of the street to reach back and open the rear windows.

Warmth pushes into the cab from the stones to his right. A cool breeze blows across him from surrounding desert air. Looking down, he sees a large raptor using the thermals to effortlessly carry it along as it hunts the canyon wall.

Soon he comes across the iconic brown signage associated with lands once under federal authority. The notion crosses his mind that the ethos attached to that federation has never been truer; now it is wholly "One nation, under God." The street sign driven into the ground at the junction of the entrance road could not be more true either as it reads, "Entrance Road."

He grants himself passage at the guard station and then follows a sign for camping and facilities further down the way. The Righting Moment had occurred during a time of the year when this area would've been nearly deserted. Still there were signs that there'd been more interest in this location than the desolate part of the trail he'd been on at that time.

Several large and obviously expensive recreational vehicles are parked neatly in a row. Provisions for electricity and sewage are connected between the vehicles, and simple junction boxes provided as a service, like crude mechanical umbilical cords.

On a large rack mounted to the back of one of the vehicles is what appears to be a motorcycle. The bike is covered by a tight fitting silver and blue cover. The man turns off his truck and walks to the bike for a closer look.

He lifts the cover and grins at what he sees. A vintage Honda "Postie" bike has been lovingly restored by its previous owner. The simple motorcycle had a cult-like following of admirers.

The bikes earned their nickname of Postie because of their use in Australia by the postal service. They are lightweight, reliable, and incredibly maneuverable. The man inspects the simple cable securing it to the RV and replaces the cover.

He returns to his truck and drives through the surrounding roads until he comes to a large maintenance building. Behind the building is a small fleet of vehicles bearing plates that showed they were for "Government use only." He parks his Humvee in front of the large bay and gets out to gain access to this building. There are no windows to break, and only a single steel door provides access other than through the garage.

He walks back to his truck and finds the Halligan bar he's chosen for just this purpose. Returning to the entrance he drives the pike at the end of the bar powerfully between the door and its frame just below the knob. He loads himself up, both hands holding the head of the tool against his chest. With a single explosive forward push, the deadbolt is broken, and the door swings open.

He walks through the darkened garage bay to open it to the light of day. He finds the large loop of chain hanging to its left and frees it from its bindings. Pulling downward, hand over hand, he raises the large steel door like a giant postmaster's desk. The full light of the day floods into the long darkened building behind him.

Turning back to face the open maintenance garage, he finds it exactly as he would've imagined. Twenty years of service for the Government teaches you that some things had become almost standard. Ahead of him, to the left, is a hydraulic vehicle lift. The corner of the bay has a tank for used oil inside of a cinderblock cofferdam, complete with a heater for burning used fluids. A neat workbench lines the rear wall with light blue Vidmar cabinets, which will certainly be filled with a broad collection of tools.

He finds a pair of long-handled bolt cutters, then opens and closes the handle to massage its rusty hinge. Swinging the tool onto his shoulder he walks back out, past his Humvee, and toward the RV Park.

Without protest, the thin cable securing the bike parts in the jaws of the bolt cutter. He runs beside the bike pushing it like a child whose bicycle has popped its chain. In the short sections of downgrade along the way he rides sidesaddle, coasting back to the garage.

With all of the tools and equipment he needs at his disposal, the task of filtering fuel and cleaning the carburetor goes quickly. He's afraid surface rust on the stator will require a good cleaning as well. However, after a few sharp kicks the little bike rattles, but for only a moment, and then answers to the throttle without hesitation.

Leaving the bike to idle on its kickstand, he walks over to the Humvee and reaches in through the window. "Come on, girls. It's time to go out and meet the day," he says as he grabs the aluminum tube.  He binds it to the top of the bike's handlebars with some wire ties he shoved into his pocket for just this purpose.

# CHAPTER 25

Pushing the bike forward, they head off to explore the ancient dwellings of the Bandelier Monument. Following the Entrance Road, around a single large switchback, he rides down the side of the mountain toward the trails into the park. He passes several structures that would've been lodging for the staff, and a large visitor's center.

He stops in front of the visitor's center. He considers that a cursory education on the people who'd lived here might be appropriate. The little bike he is straddling, and the thrill of just being out in the day, motivates him to just keep going. He makes a note to explore the displays properly before leaving the park.

Entering onto a well-established foot trail, he passes a sign that reads, "Foot Traffic Only." He cuts sharply around a steel post, placed to impede vehicles from entering, and winds on the little bike's throttle. Ahead of him he sees a circle of stones, it's center exposed clearly despite the tall grass surrounding it.

He pulls to a stop and looks into what at first appears to have been a large cistern. Perhaps it was a holding tank for storing water from the nearby stream to carry the tribe through droughts. However, a moment's further consideration shows him that the round structure could not have held its water. He smiles to himself, saying under his breath, "pun intended."

Years earlier, while first "putting on his anchors" in the Navy, he'd gone through an initiation intended to be a trial of acceptance by his new peers. During this process, he'd gone on a weekend getaway to a team building camp with the other new E-7s. The camp had a vast network of high-ropes courses, problem solving obstacle courses, and a circle very similar to the one he's looking into now.

The stone ring at the team building facility was built surrounding an impressive fire pit they'd light in the evenings. The initiates and mentors alike would sit in the circle to physically remove the boundaries of seniority. It was a sanctuary from the protocol of authorities' structure. In this circle, all people were given equal voice and allowed to speak freely.

He stands for a moment looking into the centuries old stone circle and simply surmises that this must've been the tribe's council meeting place— the spiritual center of their community. He notices that the ring of stones shows two distinct periods of building. The community must've once thrived, and an expansion of the original meeting place had been necessary.

Straddling his motorcycle, he scans the valley the ancient ruin. The steep cliff walls to his right stand out in the bright springtime sunlight. They reflect a warm, sandy beige color with sparse evergreen shrubs filling the base. Tall pines have found purchase to thrive in the many cuts eons of falling rains have cut through the valley's walls.

The caves, both natural and manmade, in the soft volcanic stone standout in sharp contrast; deep shadows fill their rooms. The effect they present is like that of the sockets in a dried skull lying on a desert floor. They project the majesty of time, even as they allure mystery in an emotionally drawing manner. He looks across the stark beauty of the cliffside dwellings and knows this is a place he will be spending some time. There are discoveries here; he feels a calm knowledge that he is where he belongs in this moment.

Behind him a thick grove of hardwoods stands on both sides of the stream that flows through the valley floor. The trees are fully wearing this season's leaves, having grown out of buds only short weeks earlier. He sees that this vein of hardwoods divides the valley in half, with the stream forming its center, for what appears to be miles in both directions.

The fact that a strong population of deciduous trees was so readily available would've tremendously benefited the people who lived here. The trees would provide not only lumber for building structures and tools, but they would provide annual mast to lure foraging animals to supplement their diets.

In many ways, this small valley is an oasis from the harsh mountains surrounding it. Those hardy souls who came to this place had been wisely led to build their lives in the ground here. It is well documented how the weight of nutrient-draining farming, combined with years of harsh drought, had eventually caused the inhabitants to leave their homes. For the generations of time this valley had been inhabited it must have been a truly wondrous place, albeit brutally harsh on short-lived bodies.

The man sees that the main trail continues up to his right, and into the core of what was once the population's center. There is a smaller trail that branches off to the left, leading into the forest beside him. His limited knowledge of the area, acquired from his short study of a Park Service pamphlet, serves as no reference as to which way to go. It is not acquired knowledge that leads him now; he simply knows the trail through the woods leads to where he is going.

Standing up on the pegs, he motors onto the smaller trail and into the woods. The gravel path shows the obvious sign of heavy springtime storms that have passed. Dead fallen branches have been culled from trees by strong winds and heavy rains. Small troughs have been cut across the trail in places by the pull of receding rain waters.

Rapid progressions of light flash before his eyes as the limbs overhead play with the afternoon sunlight. Like the trance inducing patterns of Burroughs's dream machine, the pulsations plant visions into his mind. His imagination feels loose in its socket, like a child's tooth waiting to bight a crisp apple.

Looking off to the cliffside dwellings, through the thin line of trees beside him, he sees a person standing there, and his attention is momentarily diverted. Braking quickly, he stands and stares intently into the line of carved holes on the hillside's face, trying to recapture his earlier vision.

There is nobody there. He knows this in his mind, yet his eyes scan ever more tightly. His vision probes into the shadows with tightly focused attention. Satisfied that the filtered sunlight had simply tricked his imagination, he turns back to the task of navigating the little bike along the storm-littered trail.

Only once is he forced to get off of his bike to pull a large limb aside that is crossing his path. Clear of this last small hurdle, he exits from the forest only minutes later. Back out into the full light of the sun, he squints up the rock face in front of him.

An arched opening in the side of the mountain stands waiting above him. An overhanging ledge looming over the alcove casts its interior into deep and impenetrable shadows. The effect fills him with both intense anticipation and a mild sense of dread. He steadies his thoughts as he investigates the route he must climb to the opening, well over one hundred feet above the canyon floor.

A series of three ladders has been erected to allow access. Without regular inspection from the staff of the park, he fears they may be unfit to safely climb. The first and third ladders are rather unimposing, each perhaps only twenty feet tall. The middle climb will be a different matter, as it spans a large sheer stonewall almost seventy feet in height. He'd been well known for his unwavering bravery at different times in the past; unknown to most was a distinct fear of heights.

He walks to the lowest ladder and begins to inspect it by jumping on its wooden rungs. He grabs and shakes it, intent on making it fail in some way. Aside from a small shower of pebbles from overhead, everything appears to be solid. Without allowing himself to overthink such a simple task he bounds up quickly to the first landing.

He looks up the length of the climb ahead of him. A mild sensation of dizziness comes over him as a small whirlpool of vertigo spins in his belly and flows through his bowels. His eyes notice a large section of the ledge above is missing, as if a giant has taken a huge bite. A rough pile of broken stones lie on the ground; their fractured edges have not one round side among them.

From his new perspective he sees a large boulder that appears out of place among the stones. In his mind's eye he rewinds the boulder's path, back up the cliffside, through the ledge overhead, and upward.

On the very top of the cliff, high above the alcove, a small pine hangs disjointedly by its roots. A section of the ground where it'd grown was gone, perhaps the result of the same storm which had thinned the dead growth from the forest. The large boulder beneath apparently had made its path directly through here, and recently, missing the ladders only by feet.

As convinced of the ladder's integrity as he could ever allow himself to be, he steps onto the second rung. He climbs perhaps ten feet to reassess that everything still seems to be in its place. Then he continues up, keeping himself as close to the center as possible and trying not to breath in too much extra weight.

Just over three quarters of the way up, he hears the rough call of a raven behind him. He turns his shoulders and sees the glossy black bird flapping lazily above the trees beneath him. He looks to the bird and says, "What are you doing here, old friend?" As he watches the bird, awaiting its one syllable reply, a large stone falls through his vision.

Whipping his head around to look up to the cliff's ledge he sees a wave made of rocks falling toward him as if a dump truck were parked out of view and releasing its load. Instinctively he pushes his head between two rungs to try to shelter his skull from the impacts, which are certainly coming his way. He tightens his grip and presses himself against the ladder, all the while looking down to the ground, which he is hopeful will stay right where it is.

A large flat rock lands across his left knuckles with enough force that it pushes his hand through the rung it is holding. A second large stone falls onto his right shoulder sending a brutal shock through the nerves in his neck, directly into his panicking mind. Hammer-like blows fall across his back as he feels himself make a small shift to the right.

In a sharp drop, the ladder slides off the stone face of the cliff then stops abruptly, halted by a small, jagged piece of rock. The respite of his terror is short-lived as the sudden stop has swung both of his feet free. Now hanging by one hand, it is his mass alone that ultimately pulls the ladder loose completely.

Falling quickly, he sees a small tree that is growing out of the rock face passing by him. He grabs onto the limb as it comes racing up to meet him. His fingers close around its base in a vice-like grip. He never even slows down as the branch's dry wood snaps off cleanly in his hand.

In a blind panic he tries to drive the broken limb into the rock as a mountaineer may try to break a fall with an ice axe. He pushes his feet against the cliff's face, which is blurring past him as if he were being pressed against a giant belt sander. All his efforts prove to do is push him away from the sheer wall and out into the open air; air that is growing louder in his ears as it builds up speed past him.

Falling freely, as if running in place, he turns his head and sees the ground coming fast to meet him. He realizes he is falling directly into the large pile of broken boulders. They rise from the ground like the dragon's teeth the Nazi's had used to force allied tanks into pinch points for easier slaughter.

He extends his arm, the branch still firmly in his grip, in a vain effort to break the fall. His arm is instantly driven behind him by the impact of the ground. Beneath him, one larger piece of stone stands like an obelisk as if left in place to serve as the monument of his passing. As the jagged edge drives into his side, the air is forced out of him carrying with it a thin haze of pink blood.

His body rolls off of the stones and he falls gracelessly onto his back. His open mouth tries to find air in a world suddenly having none to be breathed. His legs flail in short, spastic kicks into the dust. He tries to roll onto his side, but a pain deep in his chest stops him.

Both of his hands seek out his ribs on his right side. The branch he is carrying is deeply imbedded into his chest. Without thought he grasps it to pull it out of him. The limb is anchored deeply, and the burst of pain that erupts from his pierced flank draws the wind into his lungs in a single deep pull.

Looking down, he cannot see the piece of wood that has impaled him. He can, however, see a widening pool of blood. The single lungful of air he manages to draw escapes in an animalistic howl of rage and pain.

The chemicals, which had flooded his body in an effort to survive, begin to quickly fade. As his vision closes in from all sides and the world turns from gray to black, he sees the raven fly by overhead. His head lies motionless on its side, eyes still open. He doesn't see the small lizard coming back out of the rocks to investigate the commotion that had sent it scurrying away only moments earlier.

# CHAPTER 26

Like a will-o-wisp leading him deeper into his own imagination, a faint thought flickers into his mind, staying teasingly beyond his grasp. He feels no pain that he can focus upon, yet his entire existence is one of misery. He tries to his open eyes; they remain rolled back into their sockets as if protecting him from a reality they doubt he can endure.

His hair moves across his face and he feels a cool touch run slowly across one eye, and then the other. An angel, speaking in tongues, is whispering prayers into his ringing ears. He wills his arms to reach outward, but even through his stumbling mind he can feel the restraints holding his hands tightly together.

He has been bound; his hands are tied together, and his arms are stretched straight above him. He fights against the bondage of this unseen oppressor, twisting out of animal instinct. A soft, yet unyielding hand pushes into his chest and a calm voice coos words too alien to discern.

He feels his thoughts circling a panic as if they are sharks with calculating black eyes, waiting for the scent of a single drop of blood. His head lulls back as a hand lifts it up the back of his neck.

Something is pressed to his lips, again the calming voice flows words coolly across him.

A warm fluid fills his mouth. The bitterness is beyond comprehension, and he tries to reject it, but a hand covers his lips. Even as he coughs to expel the liquid, more is poured into its place. He gasps for air and then swallows.

After swallowing several deep mouthfuls of the horrid concoction, his torment ends. Sweet spoken words, as if dictated from his own imagination, float across him. He can feel the warmth of her breath. He can feel the glowing color of the spirit hovering over him. His traumatized senses can discern his surroundings, yet still cannot will the proper responses to his un-answering body. He feels like a prisoner trapped within himself, seeking to scream out as if in a silent, sweat-soaked dream.

Again cool touches bathe his face and shoulders. A wet rush across his chest is followed by a renewed signal of pain from his injured ribs. However, everything is growing somewhat removed, as if he were experiencing his own thoughts and feelings from a movie he'd once watched as a child. There are kisses on his forehead, on his cheeks, on his lips.

He hears a helicopter coming in the distance, its chopping blades pushing sounds to announce its arrival. The beating noise is met with a series of beeps, like a busy signal from an old phone left off of the hook. The higher, electronic warble fills the boom of the increasingly growing throbbing chop, playing in between its rhythm like a guitar strumming a crazy fingered upbeat.

The sounds grow into a power in his mind that becomes unavoidable. He yells out to the incoming assistance but hears his voice escape as a slow and low moan. A pull at his side signals the arrival of salvos of pain shooting out of his side like a broadside volley from a passing man-of-war. He arches his back powerfully to escape the torment, but someone is straddling his chest and is intent on carving him open.

Suddenly his mind is awakened, and his eyes dart open – widened pupils pulling in from the gloomy darkness. A figure is above him. Long hair spins as she dances; songs of prayer fill the air. Tubes of neon pink and green spiral though the space around her and then pop in a flash. The darkness that replaces the bright light spreads out like smoke from afternoon fireworks.

She descends upon him, cooingly, lovingly. She reaches to that place on his side where a fountain of bright red and orange flames of pain pours out. She reaches into him, tearing him, cutting him, singing softly to him. The confusing torment is beyond control and he yells out into the deep, echoing valleys of his mind.

The sound of his own voice is interrupted as his diaphragm cramps powerfully. He opens his mouth to protest, but a stream of burning bile erupts from him; his head is held to the side. Again, and then a third time, his stomach repels the contents forced upon it. She turns his heads as he struggles to regain his breath. She kisses his fouled lips and lovingly wipes his face with cool water.

The helicopter passes unseen overhead, and its deep bass chop through the air grows quieter by the moment. The figure above him has relinquished her straddling position and busies herself with some unseen task.

He exhales slowly allowing fatigue to outweigh the battle against it. Sleep comes out of the shadows and lies down quietly beside him; its purr lulls him to join it. A peaceful end of his torment settles across him and, in the corners of his mouth, he almost smiles.

# CHAPTER 27

The morning finds his weary ears; a jay squawks at its neighbor. The sun makes its way to his eyes through closed lids. His first thought is of the vision he'd experienced of love holding him as he slept, speaking to him in the tongue of angels.

This thought is quickly pushed aside by the feeling that his head has been placed in a vice and the handle turned once too tightly. He opens his eyes and sees the white rectangles of a suspended ceiling. He turns his head in confusion and sees he is inside of the visitor's center he'd passed when entering the park.

Beside him, on the ground, sits two green army canteens. His lips feel as if they have been glued closed by improperly mixed fiberglass; the taste of his own mouth offends him. He reaches for the first canteen, sitting up shakily to drink its contents.

Though warmer than he desires, the clean water is desperately needed. He drains the first canteen then drinks deeply into the second one. He rolls onto his side then finds his way onto his knees, allowing his head to establish enough equilibrium to stand. Once his mind has balanced slightly, he rises to his feet.

He walks to a large windowsill, complete with the ventilation system that would once have helped control the environment within this building. Upon the windowsill is a collection of bowls, each filled with rags soaked with a disturbing quantity of blood that he knows is his own.

On a small wooden tray next to the bowls is a hobbyist knife, and the blade from a hacksaw, which has been wound with brown twine to form a handle upon it. He picks up the crude tool and sees white grains of bone dried between the saw's teeth with a binding of blood; he replaces the saw onto the tray.

Continuing his inventory of the items laid before him, he attempts to form some comprehension of what he's just endured. A small metal bowl, one that is obviously military surplus, has a film dried into its bottom that looks like algae from a neglected koi pond. There's a small bag next to this bowl with a drawstring sewn into the top. He opens it and pours its contents onto the windowsill.

Out of the bag rolls several small green balls that are awkwardly shaped like little pumpkins. He picks one up, and at its crown is a small white flower. Though he has never seen peyote in person, he instantly recognizes the small hallucinogenic cactus. He instantly understands the vague memories of vomiting, of the dancing colors around a singing angel. Someone had dosed him with an explosively powerful quantity of mescaline.

Placing the peyote button down he sees there is a handwritten note on the windowsill as well. He picks up the paper and opens it. On the page he holds is a cryptically written series of letters and numbers. Even had it not been sitting atop one, he would've instantly recognized it as reference to book, chapter, and verse of text from a Bible.

He looks over to the corner of the room and sees that his pants and boots have been neatly placed there for him. He is pleasantly surprised to see a clean, new pair of thick socks has been placed into the neck of one of the boots. He steps into his trousers then laces on his heavy boots. Then he places the folded note into his pocket, and he walks out the door into the late afternoon sun.

Once outside he looks to his left, and the little red motorcycle lies half on its side. He sees that the only reason it has not fallen over completely is because two long branches awkwardly support it.

He steps closer and marvels at the simple ingenuity with which someone has devised a sled behind the small dirt bike. It apparently dragged him to this building. How he'd been removed from the ledge is still a mystery.

A short distance away is a bundle of some creative construction. He walks to it, drawn by both its curious appearance, and the fact that the tube containing his daughters hangs beside it.

Although someone has most obviously saved his life, they've also touched his girls; a brief flash of resentment rises up, then passes quickly. He lifts the tube from its place on the tree and says, "What have I told you guys about talking to strangers?" Then he turns his attention to the object.

Though not specifically educated in matters of the relics of indigenous people, he recognizes the hanging object as what would be called a sacred bundle. In the movies of the last century, the portrayal of the American Indian was slanted, and the naming of such a spiritual offering may have been called a medicine bag. He grasps it carefully and brings it closer to investigate it further.

The package is made of green material, olive drab to be precise. Obviously of military surplus judging by the rip stop manner of its weaving. Leather and copper wire have been used in tandem to bind it together. Loose bunches of what appear to be palm fronds have been bound outside of the main contents of the satchel. Protruding from the corner of the binding is a piece of white wood he recognizes as the branch he'd clung to; the same one which became impaled into his side.

He grasps it and allows it to slide from the confines of the bundle's restraint. Once holding it in his hand, looking down upon it, he feels the large mechanisms of panic within his mind again slip their clutch as clarity overcomes him. The "branch" that had protruded from him has an organic and readily known identity to him. He looks down at the binding of bandages surrounding his chest as reality settles upon him like a rockslide in his mind.

Holding the "branch" in his hand, he stumbles quickly back into the visitor's center and walks to a large, mirrored display case. With absolutely no regard for the timeless treasure, undoubtedly reproductions anyway, he brushes aside everything from the shelves. He sees himself clearly now.

Hurriedly he pulls away the wrapped gauze. He looks down to the place on his side where he'd been impaled and sees a large dressing, held in place by duct tape. Not bothering to give himself the courtesy of counting to three, he rips the tapings off.

There, on his side, as tidy as could be, is a thin pink scar. He recognizes how quickly he now heals, but can see that the wound is several days old. Along the length of the scar bold black thread stands in sharp contrast to his tanned skin; neat stiches have been applied to him in his mindless absence.

He turns his gaze upon himself in the mirror and raises both arms. The image he sees floods his mind with symbolism and coincidences beyond his ability to immediately comprehend. He is transfixed by his own reflection.

Standing before himself he sees a gaunt, bearded man, his arms outstretched as if forming a cross. On his right side, at the base of his ribs is a wound, which cannot be mistaken as other than the fifth wound of Christ; stigmata. The scar on his side clearly representing the piercing of the lance of Longicus, which told of the passing of the Christ.

He turns his attention to the "branch" in his hand and sees it for exactly what it is. His left hand moves to the scar, and despite its tenderness, he presses deeply exploring the wound. There is an empty pocket where once one of his floating ribs had sheltered his lungs. Again he looks to the "branch" as a tsunami of recognition sends his lesser thoughts running down the alleys of his mind. In his hand he holds his own rib, removed by his godsend of an oppressor.

He walks slowly over to the windowsill containing its eclectic blend of ingredients and places his own rib next to the improvised saw which had removed it. His mind does the rough algebra of reason as he connects the symbolism too apparent to deny. He had suffered a lethal blow to his right flank, given a rib to meet a partner, and now stands on the precipice of a new life's boldest discovery.

His hand crushes his pants pocket from the outside to confirm that the note is still safely within it. Then again he walks outside, even as the day grows darker. He is headed up the hill to the place where he left his Humvee, and the Bible he can read which awaits him in the bag on the floor inside of it.

Walking up the hill, toward his vehicle, he looks up to the moon, now showing through the collecting darkness above the ridgeline before him. The moon, only days before full when last he saw it was now in a waning phase, having passed through full without his notice. He now knows that since his fateful trip up the ladder to the Alcove House, at least six days have passed.

Coming to the small parking lot in front of the maintenance garage, he sees his trusty vehicle. He walks to the passenger's side and opens the door. Inside of the truck, in the messenger bag where he left it, sits the Bible he took from the church in

Pennsylvania. He fishes the small notepad from the bag along with the blue "Skilcraft" pen he'd collected earlier.

He climbs to his familiar place on the hood, with his back against the windshield, and pulls the encrypted note from his pocket. Still able to easily read in the growing darkness, he looks to the artfully written text of the message:

"(1)2Ty3:1-6/(2)1Th5:2/(3)Mw16:28/(4)1Jh4:8/(5)Ps107:30"

He turns from page to page, one book of the Bible to the next, deciphering the message's words. When he is finished with the task he stops, and under the moon's bright light, he reads the words he has transcribed:

*(1) This know also, that in the days perilous times shall come. For men shall be lovers of their own selves, covetous, boasters, proud, blasphemers, disobedient to parents, unthankful, unholy. Without natural affection, trucebreakers, false accusers, incontinent, fierce, despisers of those that are good. Traitors, heady, highminded, lovers of pleasure more than lovers of God. Having a form of godliness, but denying the power thereof; from such turn away. For of this sort are they which creep into houses, and lead captive silly women laden with sins, led away with diver's lust.*

*(2) For yourselves know perfectly that the day of the Lord so cometh as a thief in the night.*

*(3) Verily I say unto you, there be some standing here, which shall not taste of death, till they see the Son of man coming in his kingdom.*

*(4) He that loveth not knoweth not God; for God is love.*

*(5) He maketh the storm a calm, so the waves thereof are still. Then they are glad because they are quiet; so he bringeth them unto their desired haven.*

⋏

That she chose to end the message with the same Psalm he'd held sacred for so long makes the hairs on his arms stand erect. Reading these words, he's able to feel something he hasn't dared to imagine for countless days; he's not alone after all. This knowledge floods his mind, the repercussion breaking like a refracted wave, doubling back upon itself, off of a jetty's stone face.

He feels both absolved and terrified by the events he knows must surely be forthcoming. Steeling himself, he grasps the tube containing his daughters tightly in his left hand. Without consideration of the recent trauma his body has endured, he jumps forward off of the Humvee's hood. Landing solidly, dust moving aside from booted feet, he stands proudly facing the oncoming night.

Without trepidation, with a purity of motion, he walks steadily back down the hill to the trail toward the Alcove House. Rickety ladders be damned. He is going to meet her. Whoever she is, she saved his body.

And in his heart, he knows she will now save his life.

# CHAPTER 28

Past the visitor's center, onto the gravel footpath, and then turning into the woods, he walks as if his feet aren't touching the ground. Once as a child, he'd hit his one and only homerun in a little league baseball game. His mind couldn't absorb the fact that he'd finally cleared the fence, and he had run the bases as if in a dream.

On that sunny afternoon, as he tried to just remember to touch all of the bases along the way, everything else had gone into a vague, dreamlike state. Now, as he heads to the place where he knows his lonely isolation will end, he feels the same way. His legs move of their own accord, the stars and the ground beneath his feet somehow combine into one seamless surrounding as it moves past him.

He looks down to his feet as he steps over a collection of small limbs left by a springtime flash flood. He can see clearly in the moonlight, the two deep marks across the ground made by the drag sled that'd brought him to the visitor's center as he clung to life. The resolve, the capability, of the person who did this for him is simply remarkable.

He stops for a moment as he attempts to clear his mind of his bombastic thoughts. A small sparkle on the ground catches his eye... there is the tiniest anomaly of the light. He kneels down, then on hands and knees, he focuses hard in the darkness to study it closer.

A centipede is passing over a small flat stone, driven patiently on its multitude of little legs. He sees the outline of the insect clearly in the filtered light of the night. In the wake of the slowly passing creature are the briefest flashes of color, glowing ever so softly before fading away.

Each and every one of the tiny landfalls of this humble being's feet are igniting some form of energy. The colors are the same as the ones he'd seen reflected by the minute filaments of his daughters' remnants as light passed through them. It is the color of magic, the color of love, and it is passing between the very ground underneath of him and this seemingly insignificant being.

He thinks the peyote is still playing tricks upon his mind; manipulating the passage of the signals through his brain. As he rises to his feet he sees two perfect prints of his own hands glowing faintly on the earth before fading away. He bends over to pick up the tube carrying his daughters then stands in the silent wooded grove and just takes in the night surrounding him.

Looking up through the limbs over his head, he gazes at the sky. As he does, a small star beneath the brightly shining moon catches his eye. The small star is moving, right to left.

As a child he'd gone out into the night with his grandfather, a man of art as much as of science. They would stand together as his grandfather turned an old telescope on a tripod to the heavens. The older man would then share his knowledge of the wonders above with his wide-eyed young grandson.

Once, they'd watched a satellite as it moved through just the right line to show itself passing high above their shared point of view. The man standing now looking up, many years older but still no less wide-eyed, had listened well to the old man's words. He knows he's now watching the passage of a satellite, dormant and existing without its previous purpose.

He continues the short journey ahead of him walking quickly. He takes a moment and looks down to his feet to see if the glimmer is passing in his wake as it had the centipede's. There is no sign, however slight, of the shimmer he'd seen earlier.

Out of curiosity, he stops and removes one of his boots. Pulling the sock from his foot he drags the tip of his toe across the ground in front of him. There, ever so gently, is a small glowing line faintly visible to him in the shadows of the trees.

In slow, deliberate movements, he moves his bare foot to write the words, "Thank you" on the ground as a simple prayer. He leans against a tree to replace his sock and boot.

Smiling to himself, he walks out of the woods and stands before the cliffside dwelling, which had proven so treacherous only days earlier. As he looks up, he feels none of the previous trepidation about scaling the ladders; the center one shows prominently as having been replaced. He parts his hair out of his face with hooked fingers, tucking it behind his ears.

The alcove is filled with a soft amber glow. It is obvious that a small fire is burning inside of the opening in the hill; the outline of the cliff gives the illusion of a giant open-mouthed grin. The grin on the cliff before him pales in comparison to his own.

He climbs the first ladder almost too quickly; coming to the ledge he'd fallen onto by bounding over the last few rungs. He pauses for a brief moment to take one deep breath. Then blowing the air out of his nose, he grabs the ladder and begins to climb.

At the top of the second ladder, he sees that it has been lashed solidly into place by a cleverly devised turn of climbing rope. He can't help but give a thoughtful nod to the notice-able capability of whomever this person he is headed now to meet. He then walks the short distance to the final rungs and proceeds up.

Standing now inside of the alcove, he can see that the glow filling the air is emanating from the small square entrance at the top of the Alcove House. He knows from the little he's read of the structure's nature that the small turret visible before him is both the roof and ceiling of the dwelling, built down into the very rock he is standing upon.

He steps up on top of the Alcove house to look down and into the opening. Even as he prepares to announce himself, he spins around as a person steps out from the shadows. His heart pound-ing against the inside of his ribs, it is all he can do to stand there grinning like a fool.

She moves closer to him, her details growing more visible as she nears the glow from the fire below. He hasn't prepared in his mind any idea of whom he might meet. Had he done so, he would've been completely unable to imagine the sheer beauty of the woman standing now, only feet in front of him; her presence makes his heart feel as if it has simply stopped high in his chest.

Ava has never looked better.

Her long blond hair is tied back from her face; a large section has come free and falls over her right eye. The effect cannot be ac-cidental as it frames her strong cheekbones, accentuating her other features all the more. Her blue eyes are as if two star sapphires are burning brightly, starving the night's sky of its beauty.

She is smiling as powerfully as he is; apparently she sees him no less disappointingly. She is wearing a long and very simple black dress that appears to have no structure, all the while project-ing simple elegance. Not certain of what to do, he dumbly holds the aluminum tube out before himself as if both asking and offering something.

She moves her right hand forward slightly and an object swings out from the folds of fabric lying to her side. He actually has to make an effort to stop the stupid dog from tilting his head as he looks down at her offering. Then, as its form becomes clearer to him, he sees she is carrying a thurible.

The object, designed as an incense burner in Catholic masses, is clearly both ancient and precious. The gold it is ornately crafted from shines as if it possesses its own sunlight even here in the soft easy lighting of reflected firelight. The relevance of the object is clear to him, and he actually hears himself softly chuckle as it occurs to him how underdressed he's been carrying his most precious gifts.

They stand taking in the moment together. The knowledge that they were destined to be together is unspoken, yet plainly apparent. That she, too, has lost children to the Righting Moment. She must've seen the significance of the tube he carried immediately and recognized what he had held on to as well.

He allows his gaze to return to her wonderful eyes and sees they are pooling with tears. Her bottom lip has the slightest quiver, and he instinctively steps forward to hold her. The touch of her knocks the wind from him in a long sigh; he hears a sound softly escape her.

They stand, locked in a lovers' embrace, and begin to laugh through the tears. He holds her neck, pulls her face to him, and kisses her cheeks and forehead. Her hand has found the base of his back and pulls him toward her with deceptive strength.

Together they know they've survived an empty world facing the challenge of believing themselves to be alone. The contact they share together is overwhelming to the point of pure blissfulness.

He looks down at her chest and sees the pennant that his daughter had worn.

His hand rises to bring the small golden heart into his hand. She makes the beginnings of the motion to remove the necklace, but he stops her and says, "No." His hand moves up her chest, across her shoulder, and onto the back of her neck. They both pull their mouths together and kiss with open eyes; it is a kiss unlike any other, and they know only that it will always be their kiss.

High above the Earth, passing through its shadow, a large collection of exotic alloys and thin metallic foils spins wildly afoul of its intended orbit. Once, only minutes before the Righting Moment, a Russian orbiter had successfully docked to the main body of this now silent space station. Having made the appropriate maneuvers to complete the docking, the pilot of the orbiter is preparing a precision burn of its forward facing booster.

The settings have been verified; the rocket will burn for exactly seven seconds. This timed firing will place the now joined craft back into their constant orbit some two hundred and sixty miles above Earth. Traveling at just over seventeen thousand miles per hour, they are, at this moment, passing over the western coast of the African continent.

The pilot confirms his orders with the controllers back on the ground for confirmation. His hand rises to the controls. As he makes the move to initiate the burn, he sees the watch on his wrist tick to 0800 Zulu. The command for the recovery burn never begins as the air inside of both the orbiter and the space station goes silent. Several form-fitting flight suits hover in weightlessness, each filled with only the whispers of dust and ashes.

Over the months that follow, the space stations orbit continues to decay. Slowly at first, then more quickly as it loses altitude all the while gaining speed. With no guidance to correct itself from handlers on the ground, now long gone, it passes through the hundreds of thousands of tiny objects that have been previously left as mere garbage surrounding the green planet below.

Each object that it strikes further degrades its structure and alters its orbit. On occasion it collides with larger objects. Each piece of debris strikes out on a new vector as if played by a skillful pool player. Through sheer coincidence alone, each following collision sets in place the next. Over time, every single item mankind has ever placed above himself as a tribute of his own accomplishment loses its battle against the inevitability of gravity's constant pull.

This cataclysm of events reached its finale as satellites of every purpose, some well-known and others clandestine, lined up like stacked air traffic trying simultaneously to get holiday travelers home for Christmas. Leading the armada's burn through a thickening atmosphere is the tattered remains of a once bold endeavor to search the mysteries of infinity with a powerful orbiting telescope.

⅄

Standing together, still holding onto a long and passionate kiss, the man and woman both instinctively sense a growing tension in the air surrounding them. They hear birds becoming unsettled and flying noisily through the woods below. A startled raven caws out its raspy call as it takes flight from its roost close to the opening of the alcove.

The two separate, although they cling still to each other's hands. Their gaze turns to the sky in unison as the glowing husk of the telescope enters into sight, no longer obscured by the overhanging cliff. In the beat of their hearts, it is instantly engulfed in a bright white flash. The initial flash is so intense, it causes them both to turn their heads out reflex.

Thin streamers break away from the main point of impact and tear across the night sky in two, seemingly impossible, divergences from the original path. The man and woman watch in rapt fascination as these two lines falter and then simply go dark. They stand in silence as two more bright flashes erupt from the points where the broken away sections have finally extinguished.

Only then does the sound from the explosion make it down to their ears. The concussion of the noise pushes the air down upon them as if it's a plunging shore break landing on a wandering toddler. Through their now ringing ears, they hear a small shower of sand and gravel cascading down the stone walls. Normally such sounds would be disheartening. Yet, somehow, the two know without doubt that they stand now immune from the world's harm, if only for this moment's observance.

One point of two following impacts is just on the horizon, far to their west. The other appears as little more than a loom much further distance to the south. The tension passes from the night as quickly as it has appeared, as silence returns.

The couple stands together, holding onto each other. With this event in the sky, the synchronicity is as real to them as the ground they stand on. They now know that they've never been alone and will always have...and always had... each other.

Without any need to communicate in words, they share a calm understanding that the world is now new. Gone is the constant static of a world built to worry, the ambient drone that had gone to his head causing so much frustration. Gone too is the needless fears of false priorities, of status and achievement, which had developed into an ache like angst in her chest.

But as much as they feel these overwhelmingly welcomed thoughts, they know, too, that they as a couple are not alone. There is no mistaking the other explosions in the night's sky as evident truth that at this moment, other couples are also staring up into the majesty of creation and experiencing the same miracle together.

They both know that the creator of infinity has once again turned his attentions elsewhere, having set back to its default the miracle of this gift that is life here on Earth. The direct control will be lifted from their lives, although the light that is God's love can never be ignored again. Their lives, and their will are free again. For He has made the storm calm, and they are glad because they are quiet; he has brought them unto their desired haven.

# Epilogue

We have come to take temporary residence in what, when time was a bit more relevant, would've been a very modern and expensive home. A stark structure of cast cement built to follow the long lines of the horizon. Large, roughly cut beams of local hardwood were cast through the structure starkly boldly contrasting its simplicity like orthopedic pins drilled through bone.

The combined effect is one that quite nicely flatters the piece of land the owner had chosen on the edge of a large and vibrant lake. The waters keep wet the outcroppings on the far bank, which look like toes on the foothills beyond soaking on a hot afternoon. It was for this reason we decided to kick in the front door and feel right at home.

In a furnace room off to the side of the basement, I found a propane generator. I was able to carry one of the batteries out of the truck and coax life out of this pleasantly simple machine in relatively short order. It took me a few more minutes to find the appropriate breakers and get everything fully online.

Now music sounds throughout the house, and a fan turns overhead just inside large French doors allowing in fresh air from the lake. If I am lucky, perhaps I can even convince the air handlers to blow cold air into the rooms tonight. And after Ava and I have officially made this house a home, we can lay laughing on a large linen bed and talk until sleep takes us as we do every night.

There is a wonderful fire pit in the center of the patio, and I was quick to bring some wood up from beneath the stairs. Already, there is a solid bed of coals on which to cook. I will roast the duck I shot earlier in the nearby town's central park and then cleaned on the counter of a cantina. I've found the abundance of waterfowl on this lake matches my style of shooting the ones sitting on the shore, so I don't have to get my boots wet to retrieve them.

I saw some fly rod tubes in the corner of one of the offices off of the main hall, and perhaps tomorrow I'll begin to teach our young son how to bring food from the water. Lining the walls from the basement was an impressive display of wines, and I've found a bottle of crisp Tempranillo. The glasses the previous owner chose are quite in keeping with everything, and I'm quickly coming to enjoy his level of wealth and taste.

It'd become my way, a leftover no doubt, to the many directions my previous life had taken me, to freely manipulate the remnants of technology left for us to use. Ava, untrusting to this day of the desires that drove man to make these things in the first place, is walking proudly about the yard naked except for a bright scarf tying back her long blonde hair. I notice that she too has found the wine stash. She is carrying something that appears to be a toothbrush holder, complete with a flower in one hole and a straw in another. I don't know which I feel more, my want for her or my love.

I settle back onto a bench cast right into the side of the home after providing myself with a rather lavish arrangement of down pillows I've pulled from one of the bedrooms we will not be using. Below the patio, Ava and our young son, Able, wade among the reeds that line the shore, exploring the wonders of nature. We have chosen the name Able as a simple word play, a double play, really. The name being the first child born to Adam and Eve, and what we know he will prove to be in the challenges he'll certainly face.

After waving down to the two of them, who smile back up at me, I turn my laptop just an inch to get the reflected sunlight off of the screen and set out to write how it is that you came to read this. Please, accept my humble apology in being able to offer little more than a few well-educated guesses to help answer all of your questions as to why.

That question will enter your mind simply out of the mechanics of your flesh; you are human and will have doubts. There can never be a single person who is free from moments of doubt and pain. Faith is the ability to see something because you believe. Fear is the ability to believe only what you see.

It is a very real knowledge to me that to every person who may one day read these words, I am inescapably, and quite literally, your ancestor. As such, in these words I shall offer you my unfiltered honesty, whatever wisdom I can cull from my own experiences, and my most heartfelt hope that you know you have always been loved.

Regarding the history of how it is that we became the ones to put this story to paper, I can offer you only the following... Certainly, you have already ascertained it is not for my skills of oration alone that I was left by default to this assignment. I have come to believe that it is, in fact, because of our normalcy, our very humanness itself.

We had both known true love, and in so doing, had truly known Godliness. But we had each in our own way allowed our attention to turn away from that love, our gaze being lured away by the distractions of lesser goals than true love's pursuit. We had both succumbed to the attachments of what the world around us preached constantly as what we should desire to obtain, when in simple truth all that had ever mattered had been ours all along.

I believe that when the time came for the rooster to call the chickens home, when all of the people were polarized between what I have come to call the "uppers" and the "downers", we just happened to be the ones closest to the median. When all that had been before me had finally run its course, the creator had chosen to reseed after plowing; if for no other reason than to see what the next season would grow.

The history of what was once my history is scattered evenly across this earth. There is so much knowledge to be rediscovered. I ask you to address every new finding along your way with an unflinching desire to carry forward this world born again guided by your heart, and led by your mind, but most of all by your love for one another.

We are, all of us, creatures made to be frail at times and surprisingly strong at others. All of us are bound by the same hopes as well as the same fears. Please, hold this simple truth as a compass in your palm to set forward a course toward only your finest, rather than allow it to turn into the tools that will tear you apart.

It is now the middle of the longest day of the year, the summer equinox. The sky is as bright and alive as it ever will be. I hope to finish the task of writing these words in time to hand them, in the form of a book, to my child by the middle of the shortest days, and I shall choose the 25th day of the last month. The irony of this is not lost upon me, as I intend to tell him that it was brought as a gift from an old soul who lives far away to the North. So, quite literally, this shall be the first gift from what I can only dare dream that you, my dear reader, will one day refer to as "Saint Nick."

I love you very much,

Nicholas Morrison